DANGER

D. Cynnbalista

DANGER

E. P. DUTTON NEW YORK

Published in the United States by E. P. Dutton,
a division of NAL Penguin Inc.,
2 Park Avenue, New York, N.Y. 10016.

Published simultaneously in Canada
by Fitzhenry and Whiteside, Limited, Toronto

Library of Congress Cataloging-in-Publication Data

Cymbalista, Debbie.
Danger : stories / by Debbie Cymbalista.— 1st ed.
p.   cm.
ISBN 0-525-24744-0 (cloth)
ISBN 0-525-48495-7 (pbk.)
I. Title
PS3553.Y47D36 1989
813'.54 — dc19

88-25655
CIP

Designed by REM Studio

1   3   5   7   9   10   8   6   4   2

First Edition

For Norbert and Paulette,
without whom there would have been no beginning.
And for Enrico,
who knew it all along.

ACKNOWLEDGMENTS

My thanks to Michael Cohen for words of support, to Selma Thompson and Melissa Mizel for words of wisdom, to Neil Brisson and Jenna Laslocky for words from across the river, and to Dino Zevi for words from across the ocean.

And thanks also to the many who will remain unnamed but who gave me inspiration and who might find recognition in the pages of this book.

Contents

DANGER

Choice

"Please, treat me very gently," I tell him and he always says, "Look, sweetie, if you don't like it just tell me, okay?" I guess I like it.

I ask him, "Do I have a choice?" and he says, "You always have a choice. You can walk out of here and never come back again." I stay.

I eat the food he puts in front of me. He has prepared a steak and the blood is not juice yet: it's still blood, raw and red. I don't eat and he cuts a piece, pierces it with his fork, and places it in front of my lips. He waits, the fork still in his hand, while I shake my head, no. He tells me, "Eat," and I can't. "That's why you have to," he explains. I can't, so I get nothing else. At 11 P.M. I get up from our bed and taste some of the cold steak. "You see?" he tells me.

He tells me to lie down and I don't know if he means the floor or the bed. The bed, he lets me understand, the bed, of course. But it's never "of course" with him, he is full of surprises and moods. One day he bought me red silk stockings: two evenings later, when I wore them (for him, for me), he shouted at me for looking like a whore. I never wore them again, but they are still in my drawer at home.

I lie down on the bed and hold my hands crossed under my stomach, locking my fingers, right thumb over left. I don't know why I do it and he demands of me, "What is this new invention? Get your hands out from under there. I want to see your hands." He says, "Turn around, I want to see your stomach." "Please, treat me very gently," I tell him and he says, "Look, sweetie, if you don't like it just tell me, okay?", puts his hands on my shoulders, yanks me up and twists me around, pushes me until my shoulders are back on the bed. "Look at me!" he orders, and I hold my eyes wide open, I don't even blink because I want him to know that I am looking at him, I am looking at him, *I am looking at him*. He laughs, "You *may* blink, you know? You can stop looking at me for a second." "I don't want to," I tell him. "Well, don't let me tell you what you have to do," he tells me, and I keep my eyes wide open, I don't blink until tears form and, finally, I have to blink to let them out. "Good girl," he says, and takes his shirt off.

He drinks Bloody Marys with twenty-one drops of Tabasco and he has to count them as he pours them in the glass (drop . . . drop . . . drop . . . orange-red and fiery hot, burning my tongue after he makes me suck his finger). He never counts them aloud, considers it to be a tasteless show, exhibitionistic. When I mix his Bloody Mary I don't count aloud either but he watches me and keeps track of the drops. If I make a mistake he always knows it. He hates mistakes and is right to do so. He tells me that he is sick of my using my youth to justify my not paying attention, my not doing things the way they are supposed to be done. He is right and, although I have stopped telling him, "I am only sixteen..." as often as I used to, I now say to him, "*But* I am only sixteen," as if it really were the ultimate excuse. "What you imply is that I am wasting my time with a teenager," he explains, lying on the bed by my side, his shirt still perfectly ironed, still stiff with starch.

"No, you are not wasting your time. I am not wasting your time either, I mean it. I love you."

"That has nothing to do with anything. I've already told you—leave love out of this. What do you know about love?" and he puts his hand on my head, pulling my hair gently and kissing my forehead, the skin under my bangs, my hair.

"I know about love," I insist. "I know when I love a man and when I don't. I can always tell, I always could."

He stops passing the velvet of his lips and the sandpaper of his shaven chin on my skin. He moves his face away from mine, far from my forehead, which is still tingling, demanding more of his presence and touch. "What do you mean you 'can,' you always '*could*' tell? How many men have you been able to 'tell' about?" And then brusquely, almost shouting, "Don't tell me! Don't answer! You know I don't like to hear you talk about your lovers! Don't ever do it again!"

"But they were not my lovers," I protest. "You know they weren't...."

"I *don't* want to know," he repeats and he is getting angry, the way he always gets when I bore him, when I act sixteen and pretend I am young. The way he gets when he has to repeat things because I don't understand or don't want to understand. I say, "I am sorry, I am sorry," hoping to circumvent his anger, and he gets up from the bed and takes a grey tie with blue squares from his closet. "I wonder when you'll learn to stop being sorry and accept the consequences of what you do"—he lifts the collar of his shirt and passes one end of the tie under it—"the consequences of what you say." He

3

pulls the corners of the collar back down and pulls the two ends of the tie back and through, shifting the tie to make sure it fits fully, that it does not show or peek through in the back. "There are many things you have to learn and I love to help you but I hate excuses"—he throws the left end of the tie over the right end and starts the loop—"and sometimes I wonder if you care at all about what I say, about what I am teaching you." He inserts the right end of the tie which has now become the left end under the knot and pulls till the knot is tight and under the bedroom light the grey looks like silver. "I care," I tell him, lying on my stomach on the bedspread, supporting my head on my hands.

"Stand up, sweetie," he asks me, very gently, very softly, smiling. I push myself up on my elbows, my bare back arching, my stomach (flat stomach, a bit concave maybe, but I like the way it looks, even if he tells me no flat stomach is ever going to turn me into a Miss Universe or even a *Playboy* centerfold, my breasts are much too small for either) rubbing against the unevenness of the green and grey patchwork bedspread. I go up to him, and he pulls me gently by my arm until I am very close to him, almost face to face. He lets go of my arm and lifts his shirt collar, pulling on the right side of the tie next to his neck, pulling so that the end of the tie slips out of its own knot. The two ends of the tie once again hang in front of his shirt, two unmoving grey ribbons at each side of the buttons. "You tie it," he tells me. "Do the knot, let's see if you have learned." It's not a challenge, it's simply his informing me that he assumes I always watch him carefully, that I learn when I should. But I had not learned, I had just been lying on the bed not learning anything: I had just been admiring his precision, relishing the ritual of his dressing.

I can't, but I can't, and I lower the collar of his shirt back in place, take hold of both ends of the tie and move them back and through, though I really do not need to do this. The only thing that is right with the tie at this moment is that it is already well tucked under the collar in the back. He grins, he almost laughs, and says, "Okay, you can skip this part," and I am afraid of his laugh because it means he does not even imagine I won't be capable of doing anything else with his tie. I take the right end of the tie and pass it under the left side and around once more, in a malformed knot. I fumble trying to put the two ends back in order, pulling the right end from under the left one, trying to dissolve the mess around his neck. He pulls my hand away from his tie. "What are you doing? Do you *know* what you are doing?" he asks, and there is no smile in him now. I love him I love him I love him.

"I thought I did know," I lie. "I looked at you carefully, but it's hard to do it when I am standing in front of you, it looks different."

"Excuses," he grumbles. "All I ever get from you are explanations and excuses and whys and becauses . . ." but he does not get mad. "Come, I'll show you once again," he offers. "Now pay attention."

I look at his hands holding the two ends of the tie and moving to make it right (around and in the back and around again and back into the embryonic grey knot), his movements much faster now than they were before. When I was lying on the bed he was getting dressed slowly, focused on the tie but still and always aware of me, sometimes lingering in his perfect movements to make sure I was watching him and, all the while, watching me, my bare back, my bare ass. Now he cares about the tie, about my learning, about efficiency. The front (the left end? the right end? I don't know, can't remember) finally slips into the knot and rests on the buttons of his shirt, perfect, broad side not too long but completely covering the shorter, narrower end of the tie.

He slides a finger under the tie on the right side of his neck and tugs on it. The knot comes undone, instantaneously and naturally, as in a well-rehearsed magic trick. "Your turn," he says as he pulls the tie from under the collar (it makes a faint "swisssh" sound of silk rubbing against cotton) and hands it to me. I don't take it right away and he hits me on the face with it, grinning, then placing the wider side of the

5

tie over my eyes. I can see under it, and don't move my head or my body. Better this than showing him I still don't know what to do. "C'mon, I don't have all day," he urges, and puts his left hand in mine, settling his grey (sometimes silver) and blue tie into it, still holding my hand to pause and kiss me on the lips. "You are beautiful when you look like you do now," he offers, and I think, "Oh, I won't be able to knot the tie, oh I love it, I love him when he talks to me this way." I ask (I know I should not ask, but my need for definitions and for compliments is stronger than my judgment), "What do you mean? What do you mean when you say the way I look like I do now?"

When I am naked in front of you? When I am afraid and I try not to show it but you can (always) tell? When I love you so much that you must be able to see it even if you don't want to. When I am naked, all but holding a tie in my hand, and now placing it around my neck because maybe this will turn you on and will make you forget that you asked me to do something I can't do; I don't believe that you will forget and I know you won't but I can never tell, with you.

"I don't have all day," he says. "Take that tie off your neck and put it around mine."

"I will strangle you," I warn him. "Fine, sweetie," he says. "You do whatever you want to me, just tie this thing around my neck first."

I remove the tie from my neck, I lift his collar, I place the tie under it, I pull the ends back and through once more. I think, "If we continue this way the collar will be worn out by the time he gets out of the house." The thought makes me giggle and I laugh silently in front of him, almost to his face. "I can't see what's so funny," he says, and I am nervous and I am giggly, and I keep on bungling with his tie, hectically pulling the ends under the collar. I can't do anything else, I hope my smile does not show, Lord I am not grinning, am I? Pulling the tie one more time he takes hold of my hands and asks me (coolly), "What the fuck do you think you are doing?" He slaps my hands. He slaps my face and I say, "No please, no please," and retreat toward the bed. He tells me, "I don't have all day. I have a meeting at lunch and I am going to be late as it is. Tonight I will teach you how to tie a tie. You'll see, you'll learn." He did not hurt me and I am standing at the foot of the bed, watching (for the third time, today) his hands folding the two ends of the tie around each other, in and out to form the knot around his neck. That evening I learn how to tie a tie.

Sometimes I cannot spend time with him. My parents come back home from their travels, bringing tales of Mafia men hiding in South Africa, of old Nazis hiding in Paraguayan jungles and in the Amazonia, carrying mangoes and naïf paintings that they present to their friends and to me. My mother cooks exotic dishes, curries and seviches, and seated around the dining room table we talk late into the night. "I love seeing you happy," my mother tells me. "I am glad to see you are at peace with your life; so many adolescents are in trouble these days. Not only in trouble with the world, but with themselves. I would hate to be away from you and know you have problems you can't talk to me about."

"I am fine, Mother, I love it here, I really have all I need," I tell her truthfully, and the maid brings in fresh papaya ice cream and green tea in almost transparent china cups. Twisting the spoon in the ice cream (here I can eat what I want) I tell my parents, "When I see you two and I am with you, I know you love me and I really care for you—and you know I love you, and I really don't mind if you aren't home too much."

"Well, I am very glad to see that you are developing normally even if we are not around a lot," my father says. "*More* than normally, Father," I correct him. "Actually, I am really amazingly and unusually smart." He laughs. "And modest," he adds to my precision. "Very precocious, very, very smart," he teases me, meaning every word of it. I love it.

With nonchalance they ask about school, glad to know it is no problem. Glad to know I am no problem. They ask me if I need more money, if I am not getting tired of wearing jeans, if I want anything from Nicaragua. My room is full of primitive soapstone animals, of three-dimensional wood puzzles that have been carved out of one single piece of wood, of postcards they send me and which I always keep and save in shoe boxes. My room is full of my parents and their world, but I am spending less and less time within its four walls.

He does not ask me about school, about my grades or about how I am doing in biology. "I am not your father," he tells me. "It's not as if I did not care," he explains, "but if I started caring and you did not do as well as you should then I would have to spend my time coaching you in biology. We've got better, more fun things to do than looking at biology books."

"Yes, of course . . . But it's still part of my life . . . I mean it's me eight hours a day, you can't just *not care* about it. Whether I am good in biology or in history might not be too interesting, I know. But my friends, you never ask me about my friends—"

He interrupts me. "I *don't* want to hear anything about your friends, O.K.? Do me a favor, stop talking about teenage problems. It's rather uninteresting." I cuddle up to him on the couch, touch his calf with my finger, make the finger glide up the leg of his brown corduroy pants. "Don't tell me about your classes and about the milk shakes after school, I don't want to know," he says in my ear. "Here, in this place, on this couch, you are mine, don't tell me about your Latin professor, I don't give a shit about him. Nor about your friends. Don't tell me about your lovers or about your friends, all right? Never talk about them in here."

"But you are wrong about the lovers!" I protest and he pushes my head backwards so that our eyes meet. He has green-grey eyes. They go well with his tie, they match his bedspread, his jacket in the morning, the cotton sheets with green piping at night. In his eyes I can always read what he thinks, what he is going to do with me, to me. Sometimes I don't read correctly, though. Often I don't, actually.

8

"I have *told* you I don't want to hear anything about your lovers!" he warns me. My head tilted back, I pull my eyes downward to look at him all the better, loving him, loving his demands, the way in which he is unique to me and I to him. I can't tell him what he does not want to hear: I remain silent and he allows me to lower my head, to play once more with the hair on his calves.

In the morning he gets out of bed without any noise or fuss, he barely displaces the sheet or the blanket. The alarm always rings at a quarter-to-seven and he shuts it off right away, letting me sleep while he shaves and showers. Then he puts croissants in the oven, sometimes English muffins, which he keeps in the freezer just in case he runs out of croissants. It does not happen often, though, he is meticulous about what is in his refrigerator, careful always to keep it stocked with what he likes and needs. He is also careful about what goes into the refrigerator: he does not want low-calorie margarine in it, and threw away the tub I bought one day; he also threw away the overripe mango I brought from home, the only one remaining after my parents had once again left town.

Otherwise he has never been against my bringing things from home along with me. Blue and white jeans, T-shirts, and a red skirt he likes me to wear, all beautifully ironed and folded by his maid whom I have seen only once and who even irons my T-shirts and socks, are in his closets. I come back to his place after school, after Cokes and jukebox music shared with my friends and the socks are there, in the bottom drawer of the bureau, lying flat, paired, each pair held together by a little fold at the top. I think it is wonderful and funny (ironed socks!) and I tell him so. "I don't see what's funny, love," he says. "You have to learn to live well. Ironed socks are part of it."

"It's still funny. It's wonderful but it's funny; nobody sees what the socks you are wearing are like, it's not as if somebody at the office will say you're a slob because your socks don't have the right crease. And can you imagine the time your maid spends ironing these socks? Hours, I am sure, and I am sure she thinks it's weird, too."

"I don't pay her to think," he informs me. "I pay her to iron what I want to have ironed. And to clean what I want her to clean. It's a fair deal—I pay her and she accepts my money. Don't you like to live in a clean apartment?"

I shrug. "I don't care. Well, yes, it's nice, maybe, but I don't really care." "'Maybe'?" he wants to know, "'Maybe' it's nice?" You have an embarrassing attitude toward life," he informs me.

"I am a teenager, remember?" I challenge him, knowing that I can tease him with the remark. He does not bother to answer, which leaves me unsatisfied and sad. But later in the night he pulls himself up from the bed, lights a cigarette and whispers to me, "I wish you would stop reminding me that you are so young." I have already forgotten my teasing and I am puzzled. It is only one hour later, as he lies sleeping and I lie awake at his side, that I remember what I have told him, and I understand what he was referring to and why he has said what he has said to me.

When I asked him why he had thrown my mango out of the refrigerator and into the garbage (*"Your* mango?"—he was surprised), he told me it was rotting away and probably already had maggots. "It was not rotting, it was *ripe,*" I argued with him, "and fruit is at its best when it's ripe, especially mangoes." "Don't contradict me all the time," he told me, and that evening he brought home a bag of rotting pears and fed them to me. I thought, "He must have spent a lot of time looking for fruit this ripe." It did not taste bad but I did not bring over any more of the mangoes, pineapples, or papayas left for me by my parents. The fruits would sit in the refrigerator at my home, rotting uneaten until the maid would find them and throw them away.

I want my friends at school to know I am in love. I want them to know I am more of a person than I was two months ago, that a man (a grown man, not a peer of mine) thinks I am worth his time. That at night under and over the sheets he tells me that I am wonderful, that he loves me, all of me, my body. That I can tell him I love him too, I can touch the skin on his stomach, can caress the few hairs on his chest, his nipples. I want my friends at school to know that when I make love to him we sometimes come together, and I try not to let myself go, try not to let myself come to prolong the pleasure and anticipation. And when I come he tells me "Shhhh . . ." not because he cares about the neighbors but because he knows everything is more intense if you control it, if you stifle your cries and let your voice scream inside your body.

I want my friends at school to know that sometimes I don't know what to do: like when I rub my face on his groin (and my whole body becomes flushed and I start trembling), and then I get some of his hair in my mouth; I don't know if I should just ignore the hairs (but they are rather uncomfortable), if I should try to swallow them (but how? they would get stuck in my throat and it would be painful and even more uncomfortable), if I should stop kissing him and take the hair out of my mouth (but I am afraid of him, what will his reaction at this further proof of my ineptitude be?).

I want my friends to know that once my day at school is over, once we have all said our goodbyes (after having drunk Cokes and milk shakes, after having eaten Milky Ways and potato chips, after having listened to "Let's Spend the Night Together" and to "Stairway to Heaven") then I do not go back to my home, to my parents and to my stereo. I take the bus that brings me to the other side of town where the man I love lives in his perfect apartment. I play his music on his stereo, and his equipment is better than anything I or my friends have ever had. He has three tape decks and an equalizer with about twenty levers. He has a gigantic record collection, he has taught me to listen to jazz and now I know what Miles Davis wants to say when the notes don't seem to follow any logic.

I want my friends at school to know that I have a man who cooks for me and cares if I eat or not. I want to tell them that he hugs me when I please him, that he calls me "love" and "sweetie," that he buys me red silk stockings, strawberries in March when I tell him I like (I love) strawberries; that he buys me the books I should read and am too ignorant to know about, that he buys me black lace panties which I am still embarrassed to wear although he asks me to; that he buys large shirts striped blue and white, man-sized shirts (made of the most incredible cotton and which, I know, cost more than ten or even twenty records combined), and which he wants me to wear when I walk around his apartment, after dinner and before going to bed, and in the morning after my shower before I get dressed.

I want my friends to know about him and me and us and our love but I have promised him that I won't tell anybody about it. He told me that if he ever heard stories about the two of us I would be sorry; he added that he did not like to threaten me but the matter was too important for me to take it lightly. He made me promise and I promised and swore and I have always kept the promise except once, when I let a comment about "older men" slip into the conversation in the schoolyard. But I don't think anybody noticed it, I hope they didn't. My friends at school think I have changed, they wonder why I don't come to their parties anymore, why I am never at home in the evening and only an answering machine records their calls. My friends at school think I am weird, a few think I am a snob or snubbing them. But I don't, I am not snubbing anybody. I just don't have the time to spend with them, and I can't possibly take him along to sixteen-year-olds' parties and spaghetti dinners, nor would he ever come anyway. Spaghetti dinners! When he stir-fries fresh Chinese peapods in the wok for me; when he buys me strawberries in March and honeydew melons in February because over breakfast once I told him I liked them; when he pours champagne into chilled glasses and lets me read the label on the bottle, makes me sip from the glass he holds (some champagne always spills and neither of us minds, champagne does not leave stains), tells me that I am not drinking from a glass but from a "flute," a "flute à champagne" to be exact. How can I ask him to come with me, how can I take him to spaghetti dinners?

And I want my friends to know that when I step out of my shower in the morning, he waits for me holding a towel open wide, and then he starts drying me with it. He rubs me softly some days, roughly some other days. When he is not gentle (when he is preoccupied, or when he is angry with me), I get to school with a tingling back and it feels sore and red but it makes me think about him all the time. One day I tell him so, I say to him, "I don't like it when you hurt me in the morning while you are drying me. Because later, at school, when I lean against the back of the chair I can still feel the towel, and my back is sore. But then I think about you and I just love you, even while I am sitting in a class where a stupid professor talks about the exceptions to the ablative rule. Then I always wish I could escape from the classroom, throw the door open, and run to your office and just lie in your arms. I don't mind how you rub me in the morning, what towel you use, I just love it, I love you."

I expect him to be bothered at my talking about school but he isn't. He just hugs me and says, "Good. Morning exercise never hurt anybody, I am sure it helps you keep your sanity during the day." The next morning he dries me with a towel which is new to me: much larger than any I had ever seen him use, grey, as big as a sheet. He rubs my back with a corner of the towel, then my hair with the center, letting the rest of the towel cover my face and my eyes. In a muffled darkness, unexpected and unnatural because it is morning, I focus my attention on the feel of him drying my legs. He rubs them, drying them briskly, then dries me between my legs, rubbing for a long time.

When the friction is too much and I start to hurt, I try to get away from the bathtub and from him, I lift my arms to remove the towel resting on my head. "Don't move!" he commands and, as I squirm, he hits me between the legs with the towel. "I said, don't move, you heard me?" and lowers his hand and the towel, starts drying my legs once again. "I want to see you," I complain. "I don't like it this dark early in the morning." He does not answer so I insist, demanding, persistent. "I want this stupid towel off my head, you take it off if you want to, or *I'll* do it if you won't!" He hits me once again and I flinch and let out a small cry (out of surprise, really, not out of pain). I raise my arms and tug the sheet off me. "Stop *it!*" I order him and I am shocked at myself. I have never spoken to him this way, I cannot predict what the consequences will be.

"Tonight," he says, "tonight when you're through with school and with your milk shakes don't come back here. Go to your home, O.K.? Do you hear me? Look at me now, I am talking seriously. You can come back in a week to take your things if you want to. Or you can come back in a week and we'll talk about what has been going on here, this morning. If you can't play the game you should not enter in the draw, you understand?"

I shake my head, stunned and uncomprehending. "The game?" I ask him and shake my head again. The large, grey towel is still wrapped around me, and I brace myself with it, suddenly an object of magic and superstition which, if treated well, could make everything work out, bring me back to where I had been a quarter of an hour ago, hot and wet from the shower, eager to walk into the new towel he had opened for me.

" 'The game'?" he mimics me. " 'The game'? What game? Well, what game do you think I am talking about?" I keep still, hoping that my silence would lead him to explain more. But he only says, "You always make me late in the morning. I haven't even had a cup of coffee and I am already late." He puts on his jacket and tugs on his tie (once again the grey-silver one with blue squares). He stoops to get his black shoes, which he always puts on with a shoehorn. He

14

stoops to get the shoehorn, which should have been hanging on the right side of the closet but is not. He puts his shoes on, all the while never looking at me, ignoring my presence and stillness, not explaining because it (all of it) is clear to him and should be clear to me. As he puts his camel coat on he warns, "Don't be late for school," and walks out of the door.

That evening I go back to his apartment. I am afraid of what I will find, but I let myself in with my key, put one of my records on the turntable (he has always said that he truly hates the rock music I listen to, that it makes his head ache and leaves him nervous for the rest of the day). I move a chair into the living room, place it so that it is in perfect symmetry with the two loudspeakers, and sit in it. I listen to "Ain't Too Proud to Beg" not thinking about anything but the words of the song and the anxiety that is smothering me like a blanket, like this morning's towel. I have not even needed to rehearse the scenario during the day, as I sometimes do when I have problems that have to be resolved. The case is simple: it just would not do for me to go anywhere else, to be with anybody else. It is not a decision: I have no choice.

Once more he manages to surprise me. He does not say anything at finding me sitting in his living room when he comes back from work. He is carrying a paper bag full of groceries, enough for two but then he always hates being short of anything and would rather overstock his cupboards and refrigerator than run the risk of missing something he wants. He puts the bag on the kitchen counter and walks into the living room to lift the pickup arm from the Rolling Stone record and to turn the amplifier off. "Help me, please," he asks of me, walking back toward the kitchen. "I think the cream container might be leaking." It is, and that evening for dessert we have strawberries (had he remembered that I like them, that I love them?) with sugar but without cream.

He tells me to stand still and walks around me observing me in every detail, taking inventory of all my beauty and of all my flaws: he does not say anything but I know what he is doing, he is making sure I am not spoiled, that I am the way he wants me to be. I love it. The floor feels cold under my naked feet but I don't move them, I don't move an inch. He tells me to stand still and I do, somehow wanting to reach out to him, to grab his jacket and put my hand in his pocket. He touches me, takes hold of my arm very lightly, as if it were an injured bird, or an antique china doll. "Up!" he tells me, and lifts my arm high above my head, reaching toward the ceiling. "Up!" he tells me and takes hold of my other arm, lifts it, and places it next to the other. "Stay this way, you are beautiful," he tells me and I feel waves of pleasure wash over me, and my arms start feeling heavy and tired.

I am standing in the bedroom with my arms lifted, standing just near the bed. If I fall, I will fall on the bed or, maybe, on the floor; I know I am going to fall soon, please let it be the bed. My arms weigh too much, more than they ever did, too much for me to be able to hold them up any longer. I begin to lower them inch by inch. I look at him, monitor his gaze and his movements. He is sitting on the bed, one leg swinging lightly over the other which rests on the floor; he is fingering an old envelope he found under the bedside table on my side of the bed. I can't tell if he is looking at me. I carefully engineer the descent of my arms. Inch by inch. Centimeter by centimeter. Suddenly I can't feel my arms anymore, from my shoulders to the tip of my fingers there is only a throbbing, heavy numbness. I let my arms fall at my sides, not caring that I won't look beautiful to him anymore, that he has not told me I could put my arms down, yet.

The rush of blood almost makes me dizzy. I wish I could lean against a wall, but there is no wall where I am standing. And I don't dare move. I have already transgressed one of his commands (I am waiting for his reaction) but I will show him that I did everything I could. I won't move until he tells me I can, he will understand that I had no choice. He uncrosses his legs and places both feet on the floor, ready to stand up. As he looks at me from below, he inquires, "So, what's happening now? Did you change your mind?" He asks, "Did you hear me tell you to move?" then leans forward to take the pack of Marlboros from his bedside table and puts one into his mouth. He tells me, "When you ask me to do something I always do it for you, right?" I am thinking about what he does for me, what I have asked from him but my mind remains blank. "Right?"

"Yes, I guess so . . ."

"I guess so? Let me see—strawberries and champagne and books and waiting up for you at three in the morning because you are busy getting stoned at one of your friends' parties—"

"I *don't!*" I interrupt, but he does not let me speak, he continues enumerating what I had selfishly overlooked or forgotten.

"Don't talk. I am doing the talking now and you'll listen. I am not asking you much, but when I ask you to do something I want you to listen and to do as I say. Because that's the way I love you. I really do, you are beautiful. So, if I ask you to lift your arms because you are even more beautiful to me that way, is it an unreasonable request? I don't think so, but you seem to think it is. You did not ask me, 'Can I put my arms down?' or bother to inquire if I minded. You just started playing little tricks on me, inching your arms down for a full five minutes, hoping I don't know what, maybe that I would be stupid enough not to notice."

"That's not it!" I defend myself. "You don't understand. What if I had asked you and you had said, 'No, keep your arms up'?"

"I told you not to interrupt," he explains once again to me. "It is very annoying when I am trying to make you see my point. Listen, maybe talking about it is not worth the effort. Maybe it's that we see things differently, we expect different things from each other. You are free to move and go where you want, I am not holding you down, I won't keep you tied to the spot where you are now. Is that better, for you?"

17

"No," I say. "No." I ask him, "Tell me where to stand." I plead with him, "I did not want to deceive you, my arms *were* tired and they were coming down naturally, on their own. I was just hoping you would not notice it but I could not help it." I tell him, "We don't expect different things from each other. I really need you, I really love you, you know that, don't you?" I promise him, "If you tell me where to stay, if you tell me what to do, I *will* do it. Promise." He lights the cigarette, inhales the smoke, exhales it through his nose.

I look at him, still, standing at the spot near the bed where he had first placed me. The blood and the strength are back in my arms, I wonder if I could ask him to try me again, to let me prove to him that I can do what he wants me to do. He stands up and walks out of the room. At the door he turns around to face me and tells me, "Put your clothes back on, it's over for today." I hold on to his words, to an unstated promise that today it's over but that tomorrow we will start again.

He surprises me on weekend mornings, puts his hand on my bare shoulders and nudges me lightly. "Get up," he says, "we have things to do today." I move my head no, I still want to sleep. I never want to wake up on Saturdays, my batteries need charging. He nudges me again and says, "I'll run you a bath." The noise of water hitting the sides of the tub is like a muffled alarm clock. By the time the tub is filled I am ready to follow him into the bathroom. On weekends he prepares hot scented baths for me, passes the soap bar slowly over my body, starting from my feet (I keep my legs straight, lifting each in turn for him to lather), covering the rest of my body upward, sometimes slowly and caressing, sometimes very matter of factly; he scrubs my back and my stomach with large sponge mitts, squeezes a sodden sponge over my hair and watches the water run over my hair and my face. He sits on the side of the tub and tells me, "Careful, don't throw water around, please try to keep my clothes dry. Don't splash, you are not a child," takes hold of my chin with one hand,

and with the other hand wipes my face with a sponge cloth. "Don't move your face so much, you are beautiful," he says.

He holds the towel open as I get out of the bath, wrapping me in it at first, later taking it off from my body and carefully drying every part of me. I get dressed while he cooks in the kitchen. He likes to prepare brunch on weekends, and even though I never like to eat in the morning he tells me that I should. That I must.

"Put your jacket on," he says, "we're going out." "Where?" I ask but he only tells me that I don't need to know, that I am perfectly dressed for where we are going, that it's a surprise. He hugs me, "You are not going to spoil it, I won't let you," takes my hand, and pulls me out of his apartment. I can never forget anything with him, he takes care of it all: he carries the keys, the wallet. I don't have to think about money or bus passes. I love it when both of us get out of his apartment on an impulse, not having to rehearse mentally the list of things I have to carry around when he is not with me. He really does not want me to have money when I am out with him.

One evening in a bar he could not find his wallet; I took a handful of bills out of my jeans pockets and said, "Let me take care of it," in a mature, savoir-faire way. He hissed across the table, "Put that back in your pocket *right now!*" and I quickly put the hand holding the money under the table, stuffed the bills back in my pocket. When we walked out of the bar he asked me, "Where is that money?" and I shrugged my shoulders and said, "In my pocket." "Give it to me," he told me, and I drew it out of my jeans and handed it to him. He took it without looking and ripped the bills in two, crossed the street to get to a wastebasket and threw the pieces in it. "Don't ever do that again!" he told me. The next day he bought me a leather jacket and a pair of leather boots. I did not have any money that week until I went back to my parents' apartment to check for the mail and for phone messages.

* * *

19

We leave his apartment and go to his car. He always buckles his seat belt and wants me to do the same. He drives very carefully in the city, slowing the car down even before the light turns amber; he drives fast on the highway, his car like a toy on an electric circuit, leaving all the other cars behind us. He talks and I listen, lulled and excited by the speed of the car and by his voice. I know all about his office without ever having been in it; I know where his English desk is, where the shelves holding his law books are (to the left of the door, as you enter the office), what kind of mugs his secretaries use. He comments on everything, mimics the secretaries' accents, asks me, "Will you ever spend lunchtime comparing nail polish colors?" and we both laugh at the idea. He says, "The only way I can stand them is if I tell them to take a long lunch every second day. And I mean *long . . .*" He tells me about his university days, about the all-male clubs, Manhattan cocktails with the boys before dinner, how he can still smell the Ivy League scent that was rubbed on him during those four years. He tells me that he always avoided anthropology classes and that I should do the same.

I still don't know where we are going but I cannot ask. He tells me that a professor asked him once, "Do you have any particular reason for wearing a tie in class?" and he answered, "One of us should, so I decided it would be me." The professor always wore yellowish sweaters with leather patches on the elbows.

The boat is in front of us and it's beautiful. "You like it?" he asks me, knowing very well that I love it. "It's ours for the weekend." I hug him from the back, my hands meeting on his chest, squeezing as hard as I can to show him my delight. I smell his hair and the sweetness of the rotting seaweed drying near the water. "I love it, I love it," I say.

He never forgets anything: he has brought along a suitcase with towels, shirts, and underwear for me and for him, a set of new toothbrushes, toothpaste, little soaps. He takes two portable coolers out of the car trunk, hands me one, and says, "Careful, keep it upright, it's full of food, don't let it spill." "When did you prepare this?" I want to know. "Where did you find out about this boat, how were you able to hide the food from me all this time?" I put the cooler on the ground and hug him from behind one more time. "Stop it for a moment," he orders. "Let me get through with this." But I can tell he is happy at my delight, at the success of his surprise.

We spend the rest of the weekend on the boat. There is nothing for us to do but make love, talk until he asks me to shut up for a while, make love again. I am so happy I can't sleep at night, so I walk up to the boat deck and sit thinking about him and watching the black water. He slowly comes up the stairs to the deck, yawning and rubbing his eyes. "What time is it?" he asks me and I say, "Three-thirty, I couldn't sleep . . ." He sits near me and keeps me warm with his body. He hugs me and he tells me stories throughout the night.

He cooks brunch and tells me, "Eat," when I tell him I am not hungry. I play with the fried eggs, mashing them down with my fork. "You *should* be hungry," he informs me. "You didn't sleep all night." I put a forkful of runny eggs in my mouth. "You should especially eat the yolk, it's good for you." "I hate yolk the most," I tell him. "That's why you should eat it," he says. He comes near me and takes the fork out of my hand. Licks my eyelids with his tongue and then picks up some eggs from my plate with the fork. "Eat!" he says again, and I open my mouth. "Good," he says, "it's all yolks," I shudder, and laugh at his teasing. He walks to the small kitchen counter, takes a coffee spoon, comes back to me with it. "Open," he says and I open my mouth once more. He spoons the eggs into it, and I let myself be fed by him, loving it and hoping that the downpour of eggs in my throat will stop soon.

He has even brought books along, one for me and one for him. When I pick up *The Gulag Archipelago* he says, "I did not bring you on a boat so that you would spend your time reading." I sit on the deck and daydream, see fishes jumping out of the water, the shadow of their shapes under the boat.

When I tell him about it, he tells me he has not brought fishing rods along because he hates the sight of suffocating fishes writhing and dying on the deck of his boat.

He starts the car and we drive back to the city: there are no more surprises for me this weekend. Sitting in the front of the car, strapped to the seat by the belt, I think I might have forgotten *The Gulag Archipelago* on the boat but I know better: he must have seen it and picked it up without telling me anything about it. I can count on him to take care of the details in my life. Later, he will ask me if I think I have taken everything along and I will lie and say, "Yes, why?" just to hear him say, "Why do I always have to take care of you?"

He warns me, "Don't look now," when I wake up and want to get out of bed. "Turn around," he tells me. "Put your face back on the pillow and close your eyes. I don't even want to see your eyelids flutter." His voice is close to my ear, I can feel the coolness of his breath on my skin, smell the mint of his toothpaste. I want to get up, open my eyes wide, see him, look out the window to see if the sun is shining as it should be on a day like this. I also want to get up and go to the bathroom and brush my teeth right away: I want to pee. But I can't, and I lie hugging the pillow with both arms, listening to the sounds he makes: I hear him opening and closing closets, looking for something that has defied and escaped the order of the apartment. He opens the kitchen cabinets, then the coat closet in the hall, the cupboards in the dining room. There is a faint "ting!" of glasses and flutes colliding, I hear him saying "Shit!" under his breath as he cautiously closes the cupboard doors. He walks into the bedroom, the leather slippers flap against the wood floor. It's always a strange, threatening sound to me: I burrow my head in the pillow, pushing deep down to let him know I am not playing any tricks on him. I breathe the hot air of my breath and wish he would come closer to me the way he is now, in his purple-black dressing gown and leather slippers, wish he'd brush my forehead with his hands and lips, wish he'd let me get up.

He turns the key of the bedroom closet and opens it. I hear him taking boxes from the top shelves, lifting their lids. I lift my head from the pillow, keeping my eyes shut, squeezing them as tightly as I possibly can to make sure he knows I am not cheating. "Please, let me see . . ." I ask him and he laughs and tells me, "You are a sight, stop making faces at me this early in the morning." "Let me get up," I ask of him. "I want to see what's in those boxes. C'mon, it can't be a secret, what are you looking for? Tell me!"

"Did I or did I not tell you it's a surprise?" he inquires. "I remember I did tell you to be quiet and not to look. So do as you've been told, you'll enjoy it, I promise."

He continues searching through the boxes, opening lids and lifting objects wrapped in layers and layers of paper. Some of them he unwraps, and I can hear the layers being peeled off, one by one. But the "Damn!" becomes more frequent, his peeling quicker and more erratic. He rips open some kind of package and the noise of the torn paper jumps into my ears. As I begin to discover the world through his sounds the sounds suddenly cease. *"Damn!"* he repeats once again and a box is thrown on the bed. "Might as well get up," he informs me, in a flat voice. But I keep on hugging my pillow, hoping that he will change his mind and continue his search: I want my surprise. "I guess you heard me," he says and walks out of the room.

I get up and look at the box open on the bed. It contains lots of waxy tissue paper, and long silk scarves, coiled into themselves like rainbow snakes. I love these scarves, and sit on the bed wondering who they could have belonged to, why they are now semi-hidden in his closet, why he does not tell me to take them if I want to, what treasures the other boxes contain. I wonder who brought them into his apartment and why. I am jealous.

I walk into the living room wearing one of the large

23

striped shirts he has given me, a black silk tie wrapped around my neck. "Good morning," I say.

"Have you brushed your teeth, yet?" he wants to know and I shake my head, no. I have forgotten in the excitement and disappointment of the day. I spin around, perform a quick retreat away from him, rush toward the bathroom: he likes me to be clean when I come to greet him in the morning. "How many times," he asks, "will it take before you start listening *and* paying attention to what I say?" Bent over the sink, I can only hear fragments of his speech. Most of his words are muffled by the foam of the toothpaste, drowned by the sound of hard bristles on my teeth.

He says "Because if I ask you . . . you think you are . . . I know about . . . and then you'll say you're only . . . here with my coffee . . . what are you wearing anyway?"

I see the reflection of him in the mirror in front of the sink. He appears framed by the bathroom door as I am rinsing my mouth, carefully swishing water around it to remove the sting of his toothpaste. He is standing behind me, holding a piece of the silk scarf between his two fingers, lifts it up over my shoulders for me to see it in the mirror. I see myself in the mirror, I see him, his hand and the silk scarf he is holding. I start wiping my mouth on my sleeve, then remember he's there and switch to my towel near the sink. "It was in the box," I offer, "the one that you left on the bed. There were lots of scarves, colored ones, but I thought black, sort of, is the most interesting . . . and anyway, why do you have all these scarves?" Somehow I dare going all the way. "Whose are they? And what's in all those boxes?" Somehow I dare making fun of him. "Is it makeup? Do *you* go around in drag?"

He lifts me from under my armpits and tugs me to the bedroom, throws me on the bed as I try to struggle free, to writhe away from him. He holds my wrists behind my back with one hand and strikes me with the other.

I stop struggling and just concentrate on moving my face to anticipate the blows, on arching my back so that he does not hit me where it hurts most. Suddenly he lets my wrists go and stops his motions, remains standing at a corner of the bed, slightly bent over my body, watching me. I am curled up on the blanket, not wanting to think or feel, wishing it weren't Saturday and I could go to school. Wishing I knew how to love him better, wanting him to tell me if he wants me to fight (no, he does not, I already know it) or if he just wants me to behave. I am also trying very hard not to cry but it's not me, it's uncontrollable, and once again this morning I bury my face into his bed, I don't let him see my eyes. He says, "I hate when you don't respect me. I love you, you know."

"Do you have a boyfriend?" my friends ask me in school. I can't give the answer I want to. I have to say, "No, but I don't want one, I'm fine like this."

At a dance Diana and Luisa motion me to come near. "I want you to meet this guy," Diana says. "He is unbelievable, and he wants to meet you." "I don't want to meet him," I reply, almost frightened by the idea. "Don't be stupid," Diana insists and Luisa butts in, "Anyway you can't not meet him. He's coming this way right now."

He is gorgeous. He is tall and blond and, smiling almost shyly, he tilts his head toward the dance floor. "Want to?" he asks.

He dances well, barely moving his feet but shifting his tall body like a reed in the wind. He moves fast and I am actually enjoying it, jumping around him, spinning on my leather boots, letting my head bounce freely to where the gravity and the centrifugal force of my motion sends it. I know we are great partners, his stillness counterbalanced by the dance I perform with him as my center. The Stones are followed by Roxy Music and then by the Who. We chant "M-m-m-m-y g-g-g-generation" in unison, and his body becomes spastic, he flaps his hands in front of his face, opens and closes his eyes rapidly. I imitate him, jolt my head toward him, almost thrusting it into his flapping hands, jerk my rigidly held arms on the sides of his body. The Who change into the Stones once again, it's "Wild Horses" and he puts his hands on my shoulders, pulls me toward him and starts dancing very slowly, following perfectly the sadness of the music.

I don't want to dance with him anymore, this is becoming more than I had asked, more than I had bargained for. But he moves so well, he fits his body against mine, removes one arm from my shoulder and wraps it around my waist. He is tall, taller than I am, and I rest my head on his shoulder, to mold better with him, to heighten the synchrony of our dance. We sway on the dark dance floor, unaware of anything but the perfection of our motion. Lost in the dance and in each other he holds me tighter and I think, "But he *is* gorgeous . . ." and let him kiss my hair, my neck.

He lowers his head toward my mouth, his lips searching for mine, and I am slapped into a realization of what's happening. I snap my head backward and push him away; turning around, I start to run away from him. I hear him call my name as I cross the dance floor, see him coming closer as I am getting my jacket, know he is looking for me and wanting explanations. He grabs my arm and I pull myself free, open the front door and rush down the hallway, run out of the building into the night of the city.

I am his and I love him, and he knows it. I tell him so, so many times each day. If he knew what I was thinking about at the dance, if he knew what I did, he would kill me. He would stop trusting me, and teach me a lesson, and kill me. I can never let him know about it, I think, but the next day I tell him everything.

The worst thing he can do is ignore me. He does not come to dry me in the morning, lets me wait until I get cold, and have to look for a towel by myself. He only puts one croissant in the oven, forgets to heat up the water for my tea. He throws away the paper after he has read it, does not wake me up in the morning, and I have to be careful to listen to his alarm clock ring because he never lets it ring very long, always shuts it off right away and if I don't wake up, I don't wake up. He does not put my ironed shirts in the closet along with his anymore: he leaves them on the dining room table and lets me take care of it on my own. He does not strike me or teach me a lesson. Or, rather, he is doing both by not paying attention to me anymore.

He unbuttons his shirt in the kitchen. He has taken the record I was playing off the stereo to listen to the news on TV and now he is not even watching it. I am not listening either, though I have remained in the living room and I am looking at the TV screen. I have not been able to think these days, I can only concentrate on the actions that are directly related to my survival. At midnight, I remember that I have to eat; after getting dressed in the morning I have to take my clothes off to wash myself and then get dressed once again. In the library at school I put my papers on a table and leave them there, walking to class without even a pen. I am stopped in the bus because I have not paid my fare: I have forgotten to pay and I tell the driver so. "Sure," the driver replies and I get off the bus and walk to the apartment because I cannot stand the sarcasm in the bus. When I get home that evening, I realize that I have forgotten my wallet at school, that I could not have paid the bus driver even if I had wanted to . . .
     He calls to me, "Come here!" and I turn my head in the direction of his voice, get up from the couch, and run into the kitchen. He is holding the shirt in his hands and says, "Try it on, I want to see how it fits you." I don't talk, too pleased to ask for any explanations, and immediately put one arm in the shirt's sleeve. "Do it the right way," he says impatiently. "Take your shirt off." He touches my stomach as I lift my T-shirt over my head, and as soon as I am wearing his shirt he reaches toward it and starts closing the buttons. First the buttons on the cuffs, then those on the front. He steps backward to look at me. "It fits you, it's yours," he says, and adds,

as if it were an afterthought, "Will you please get my cigarettes?"

He walks out of the apartment to buy strawberry ice cream, strawberries, and lace cookies. Back in the kitchen he puts the strawberries, sugar, and cream in the blender and prepares a sundae for me. He feeds me on his bed, telling me when to open my mouth, when to lick the spoon, when to kiss him. He puts his finger in the pink cream at the bottom of the bowl and draws strawberry lines around my mouth, takes my shirt off and paints strawberry circles around my breasts.

"Enough ice cream, please," I say and warn him, "I will get fat . . ."

"Let me be the judge of that, this stuff is good for you. Don't you like it?" (I nod yes) "So don't worry, I'll take care of you, I'll make sure you don't get fat, trust me. Now be good and open your mouth." I open my lips just enough for the teaspoon to slip through, mixing the strawberry taste with the smoky taste of his mouth in the kiss that follows.

The report card comes in and I make a Xerox of it to send to my parents in Lima, Peru. He asks me, "How did you do?" and I am stunned that he asked. He surprises me, he always changes the ways he cares for me, the ways he loves me: he tells me not to wear anything when I am in the apartment, he pulls his sweater over my head, wraps my shoulders with his jacket or, he says, I'll catch a cold; he orders me not to eat anything (I am really too greedy), he feeds me eggs and ice cream and chocolates filled with cognac; he demands to know where I have been, what I have done when I am not home by the time he comes back from the office, he tells me I can do what I want with my time; he does not let me tell him anything about my school, my grades, the food fights in the cafeteria. He asks me, "How did you do?" and wants to see my report card.

"You don't want to know," I laugh. "It's not the best-looking thing in the world." He orders "Hand it over here,"

28

and I shrug my shoulders, open my school bag and give the card to him. He raps the back of my hand with the TV remote control that was on the table in front of him, tells me, "This is disgusting!" and I protest, "I didn't know you cared."

"I care about *all* you do, sweetie," he says, "and some day you'll finally understand it." He hands the card back to me warning, "Never let me see something like this again!" "The card or the grades?" I want to know. He walks out of the living room and does not answer.

The first time he tied me on his bed I was maybe a bit afraid, but he said, "Trust me, I know what I'm doing," and so I trusted him. He does not need to ask me to trust him anymore. But still, sometimes, as I look at his face, at him towering above me, I melt in a pool of want and fear and anticipation. I lie waiting to know what he will do next, and he bends so that his face touches my body: sometimes he kisses me and sometimes he bites me. I can never know which it will be until I feel the wetness of his lips and tongue or the sharpness of his teeth on my skin.

He moves on me and with me. He says I am beautiful when I can only move as I do now, when I don't make noises when I come. He has kept the box with the coiled silk scarves under the bed: he teases me and does not let me choose the colors I like. He asks, "Which one for your hands, which one for your mouth?" and when I decide which scarves I want he tells me I have no taste and that he's going to do the choosing.

I don't even have to ask him to treat me gently anymore. He always does, and if he does not, he then explains why. He sits patiently on the side of the bed, smoking and shaking his head, hurt by my refusal to understand and by my stubbornness.

"If you don't like it, you can ask me to stop."

"But you wouldn't, you never stop when I ask you to, my asking would not make any difference. Like when—"

"Let's not start with the 'like whens.' There is nothing I hate more than a woman who says 'like when' or 'I told you so.' You probably don't realize how annoying it can be to listen to you lying on my bed and whining 'like when.' Annoying and unappealing. Stop it."

"But you wouldn't stop even if I asked you—"

"That's because I know you don't really want me to stop, that you will enjoy it. I know what you like, don't I?" He waits for me to answer and then fills the gap of silence. "Yes, I do. You know it's true, you're just too proud and stubborn to be honest with me and with yourself. I can't stand it when you lie to me." He gets up from the bed and turns toward the door.

"Wait," I ask him, "don't go!" He walks out the door and I call, "Come back! Please come back! Can you please come, please?" I try to take the scarf off my wrists but only manage to twist my fingers close to the knot. I struggle with my hands and the knot becomes tighter, the silk transformed into a rope. "It's *hurting* me!" I say once, then once again, louder and louder. He comes back to the bedroom eating an apple and stands at the door looking at me. "Stop clamoring," he orders. "What's the matter with you today?"

"Please let me go," I ask once again and he is silent, chewing. "Please could you untie the knots, it really hurts," I say, and he tells me, "Say please."

"But I just did, I asked you please to let me go, please, the scarves, the knots, are tight, they are hurting me."

"And just *how* did they get that way?" he asks, still leaning against the door frame, still slowly eating the apple. "You got them that way yourself, didn't you? And now you want me to help you get out of one of your messes . . ."

He comes close to the bed and tells me, "Say please," and I say, "Please." He tells me, "Say I beg you," and I say, "I beg you." He tells me, "Say I am sorry," and I say, "I am sorry," and I say, "My wrists, they are *hurting* me, please let me go."

30

He tells me, "Next time you start fucking up I might not be around to help you, remember that," and tries to untie the knot of the scarf at my wrists. He has to cut it open with a kitchen knife and, once all the scarves are loose, he kisses my wrists and ankles, makes me take a bath and then dries me, hugging me with a towel in his arms.

"I'm not going to college, I'm not going away from here," I tell him. I cuddle up against him, and he passes his fingers through my hair. He lets a finger slide down my head, behind my neck, he follows the outline of my ear, and whispers in the air, "Darling, little one, don't talk about it, shhh . . ." I tell him, "I never want to leave you," and he asks me, "You don't, you really don't?"

I start crying and I don't know why. I hold on to his shirt with all my strength, grab his arms, and hide my face in him. I breathe his smell, the recipe that I love, the faint lingering mint of the morning toothpaste, the alcoholic pungency of his aftershave, the tobacco on his breath, the mildness of his almost imperceptible sweat. I cry and I say, "No, no . . ." I catch my breath and I repeat to him, "I love you, I love you, never let me go . . ."

He continues to stroke my hair, to massage my neck. He cups his hand and places my chin in it, removing my head from his stomach. He licks the corners of my mouth with his tongue, the sides of my nose, my eyelids. He tells me, "Darling, love, stop crying." He tells me, "Don't worry, little one, I promise you, I will never let you go." And I look up into his face and ask, "It's a promise?" and he tells me, "Yes."

Manhattan
Boxes

Contents of Peter's refrigerator:

One bag of ten limes from the Korean greengrocer
One bag of ten lemons from the Korean green-
   grocer
Two bottles of Cuervo Especial Tequila
One liter bottle of Cointreau Bleu
One liter bottle of Triple Sec, orange
Several jars of Caviar, one large chunk of Parmi-
   giano Reggiano, jar of Calamata olives, jar of
   martini olives, jar of cocktail onions
Champagne, Veuve Cliquot and Mumm, both
   cuvée 1985
Crock of Pommery mustard
One orange in the fruit bin

When Peter walks out of his apartment he turns the key in the top and the bottom locks then checks them both. There is no guard or doorman in his brownstone so he had a steel door installed before he moved in. When one of his girlfriends wants to sleep late—and he has to leave for work at 7 A.M., trading starts at 7:45 A.M. sharp—he spends the day in a state of suspended anxiety. Will she remember to close the upper *and* the lower lock? Will she check the door? Will she check it twice? Will she then lose the keys? Will she ever return the keys or, rather, will she turn them over to her next partner, certain to be a vindictive and jealous man?

Peter only feels at ease when he comes back from work and finds his apartment in its usual state: a comfortable state, where the leather couches are thick, the books are hardcovers, and the few paperbacks do not fall apart at the binding. Where socks are matched in their drawer and towels do not lie on the floors, where the blender for margaritas does not leak and there is never any danger of the cheese getting bad: wrapped in a moist towel Parmesan can keep almost indefinitely. You can, Peter says, have a class act even if you are never home. He serves large margaritas, generous chunks of Parmesan, and olives to his guests and lovers.

Lydia tells Peter: "If I didn't know you I'd think you were a caricature."

"You flatter me," says Peter.

Contents of Lydia's refrigerator:

Six-pack of Miller Lite, minus one can
One jar of honey roasted peanuts
One container of take-out sesame noodles, very
    spicy
Half a Sara Lee strawberry cheese cake, in original
    pan
Pepperidge Farm chocolate chunk cookies
Famous Amos chocolate chip and pecan cookies
Diet Pepsi
Crock of Pommery mustard

34

By now Lydia has been seeing Peter for four months already. When they first met she told him she did not believe in monogamous relationships. "Neither do I," said Peter. She liked his honesty and felt slighted.

"How can I know," Lydia asks Peter, "that you don't have herpes or AIDS or God knows what when you sleep around so much?"

"I trust you, don't I?" answers Peter and so Lydia does not bring the subject up again. She thinks about him a lot; when she first met him she was almost in awe of his apartment, of the continuous supply of champagne in his refrigerator, of the 100 percent cotton sheets on his bed. She is jealous of the strangers who sleep with him, she worries about AIDS (though she screens her lovers carefully, she is not sure Peter does the same), she worries about being as sexy as his other lovers surely are, worries about sounding like a paranoid prude if she were ever to bring up the subject of AIDS again.

Peter and Lydia met at a bookstore in the Village. Peter was looking for an out-of-print book about Cezanne, Lydia was looking for cheap books as Christmas presents. She had an interesting body, small with broad shoulders, no bulky parka or down jacket hiding her thinness. Peter tapped on her shoulder and asked, "Are you sure you want to buy a Norman Rockwell book?" and she said, "It's for my mother and it's none of your business, anyway."

"You have to teach things to your mother," Peter instructed her. "Don't let her drown in the Rockwell sea of life. Let her know about Cézanne, Stella, Bacon . . ."

He was a conceited son of a bitch, Lydia thought. She said, "Why? Is that what your mother reads?" and in a flat tone Peter answered, "No, my mother's dead." Without wanting it, knowing that nothing changed the simple fact that a stranger was being condescending to her and that she should simply tell him to fuck off, Lydia felt sorry for Peter. "Oh . . . and when did she die?" she asked.

"I don't know. Something like six years ago," Peter said. And though this was not the answer she had expected—its imprecision, the nonchalant manner in which the information had been delivered almost shocked her—it was too late. She was already attracted by the misery she presumed he felt, by his aggressive cultural come-on. So when Peter suggested they have a cappuccino together she was unable to forget he was an orphan and walked out of the store with him. She did, however, buy the Rockwell book. Now, after almost half a year, Peter still reminds her about the book and teases her about it.

Lydia eats at Chinese restaurants and asks for doggie bags before paying the bill: Peter says the whole concept disgusts him, makes him feel like a beggar, like a dog asking for table scraps. He refuses to eat with Lydia if she is going to ask the waiter to let her carry home her own garbage. "Fine, sweets," she told him, "if you take me to the Four Seasons I promise to eat everything on my plate, have no leftovers and ask for no doggie bags." They have never gone to the Four Seasons and Lydia eats at Hunan Empire with Jean-Jacques.

Contents of Jean-Jacques's refrigerator:

> Seventeen rolls of Kodak 1000 ASA black and white 35 mm film
> Five rolls of Agfa 35 mm color film
> Eight four-packs of alkaline AA batteries
> Boursin aux Fines Herbes, Boursault, large chunks of Gruyère, Gouda, and Stilton
> Two opened cans of Alpo dog food
> One jar of hoisin sauce, one jar of capers, one jar of green olives, one jar of sun dried tomatoes, one jar of kosher pickles
> Perrier, skim milk, and grapefruit juice
> Crock of Pommery mustard, jar of Moutarde aux Fines Herbes, jar of Moutarde de Dijon, jar of Japanese green mustard

36

Jean-Jacques has never met Peter. Judging from what he has heard about him he does not care to meet him either. "What kind of man," he asks, "would refuse to share dishes at a Chinese restaurant?" From across the table his chopsticks plunge into one of Lydia's wontons, pierce it, and lift it up in the air as if a war trophy. He chews on the trophy. "Where do you find all those weirdos, hon? Why does he even go to a Chinese restaurant, then?" Once more his chopsticks fly across the table and land in Lydia's plate, pierce the hard fried skin of the dumpling. "What's this guy do? Is he an investment banker?" "Almost," Lydia whispers, lying. Peter is—no doubt about it—an investment banker, and she knows it very well.

Jean-Jacques asks Lydia, "Mind if I take your last wonton?" Lydia shrugs her shoulders and Jean-Jacques's index finger and thumb land in her plate and smear the oyster sauce. Lydia looks down at her plate and then at Jean-Jacques's face, watches him frown in concentration as he tries to grab the wonton—the sauce and oil have rendered it very slippery and greasy by now. She thinks Peter might have a point, after all.

Jean-Jacques's fingers finally manage to grab the wonton. As he chews on it Lydia pushes the empty plate away from her.

"Do you want some broccoli?" Jean-Jacques offers.

"I'm going home," Lydia tells him, and Jean-Jacques tells her, "Let me take you home." Lydia looks straight at Jean-Jacques, at the black muffler he perennially wears around his neck, at his aqua blue eyes hidden behind incongruously thick John Lennon glasses; for a very brief moment she evaluates her possibilities, and chooses Peter.

"It was awful," Lydia tells Peter. "He was sticking his fingers and chopsticks and everything else and God knows what in my plate all the time . . ."

"Did he," Peter asks seriously, almost severely, "take any food home?"

"I don't know. I left before he did."

"Good thing you did not have to stay there to watch him wrap the meal up," he tells her.

"If I weren't here with you I'd be carrying a full half-eaten portion of spicy Chinese broccoli home," she challenges him.

Peter looks at her and smiles. She cannot tell whether he is smiling because (even though they have known each other for months) he still does not believe she really would, because he is mocking and being condescending to her, or because he finds her candor endearing. It's all one and the same, thinks Lydia and asks Peter, "Will you ever take me seriously?"

She is content when he hugs her and then steps away to face her, still smiling and silent. She tells him, "You are so dimensional and so much more, oh, I don't know... disjointed than you ever let yourself seem," but Peter shrugs the compliment off. "Don't believe it," he says. Lydia does.

At Hunan Empire, as the waiter slides the remains of plates of broccoli with cashews and sticky rice into the Chinese doggie bag, a white cardboard container, Jean-Jacques carefully folds a paper napkin around three fortune cookies and pockets them. In the subway he breaks the cookies open, reads the messages, and throws them away along with the crumbs. As always, after a Chinese meal, he wonders about the life of the fortune cookie writer: Is he an idiot or a Confucius in disguise? Does he exist at all? He imagines the Guild of Fortune Cookie Writers meeting in a basement in Chinatown, exchanging greetings and two-line words of wisdom.

If Jean-Jacques is in love with Lydia he certainly does not let it show. Mostly—his friends have by now concluded—he does not fall in love with anybody. He does, however, take great pictures of SoHo Buildings.

Sometimes when he feels depressed he asks Lydia to pose for him, places her against a wall and yells, "Stop smiling!

Stop smiling, just pout! Pout! *Merde de merde,* what do you want to do, do you want to spoil the whole *effect?*" Then Jean-Jacques —the camera continuously glued to his right eye—walks backward, farther and farther away from her. Away until he can be sure that Lydia's expression will not show or be recognizable in the final product. Jean-Jacques does not trust himself with live subjects. He has not yet discovered, he says, how to make humans seem just as static as the buildings behind them and yet show they have life in them; he is afraid that their intrinsic motion and fleetingness will show through.

"Because," Lydia explains to Peter, "it all boils down to this. He is afraid of motion, never wants things to change in his pictures, in his life."

"That's a lot like me," Peter tells her and Lydia is surprised and rectifies him, "Don't be stupid. You *do* things, you like things to change around you, you're always in motion."

"My motion," Peter says, "is only a fight against entropy. I move to keep things the way they are. Or the way they were, rather."

"You are so pompous," Lydia says and does not change her mind or say she is sorry even though she sees that Peter is hurt by her comment.

The men in Lydia's life are: Jean-Jacques as a wonderful friend and nothing but; Dan as a wonderful lover and nothing but; Peter.

Contents of Dan's refrigerator:

Pizza—very old, curly; one orange slice at bottom of box it was delivered in; peppers and mushrooms missing from top
Two bottles of Dos Equis beer
Jar of Grey Poupon mustard

Dan invents games for him and Lydia, and she loves to play in them. They enter their roles with almost no talk and no explanations; they hide the tangibles of everyday life from each other, lie and pretend they know each other much less than they actually do. Ultimately, the gift of their feigned ignorance is freedom.

"I don't know any of your friends," complains Dan while the grey light of January early morning chills his bedroom, flattens the curves of their bodies (still moist after their sleepless night), robs their skin of translucency, making it look dry and powdery. "I don't want you to," Lydia says. Lydia never eats breakfast at Dan's. Not out of choice but out of necessity: there is never any food in his refrigerator. "But," Lydia tells Jean-Jacques, "even if there were any I don't know that I would eat it. I mean, the place is so anti-hygienic, for God's sake!"

"Then how can you sleep there at all?" Jean-Jacques wants to know.

"I don't know... I guess it's different, he's a clean person, I was not talking about him but about his place. I mean, his pad is like so... minimalist but not funky-minimalist like New Wave—style, no, it's not some kind of statement, it's just minimalist-empty, he's really got *nothing* in there. No furniture and nothing to eat but somehow roaches still find their way to his place."

"Charming."

Lydia pouts. "It's not a question of 'charming.' And eating there or making love there is very different, but you men don't understand it."

"Now," Jean-Jacques admonishes her, "don't be a bitch. Don't give me that feminist jive." Momentarily Lydia hates him, but when Jean-Jacques (almost pleading, almost demanding a favor and a gift from her) tells her, "Don't hate me," she feels close to him again.

It was bound to happen and it does. Lydia and Peter are waiting on line at Balducci's; four croissants, a jar of English grapefruit marmalade, and a block of fresh cream cheese are lying at the bottom of their basket. Breakfast things for tomorrow morning. Lydia feels a tap on her shoulder and, be fore she is even able to identify the hand, she hears Dan's voice. "Hey, what'ya doing here!" he says loudly and Lydia impulsively grabs Peter's coat sleeve and holds onto it like a child about to lose her mother in an amusement park crowd.

"Hi, Dan," Lydia says in a flat tone.

"Haven't seen you in a while, kid." He is joking, they had actually met over the weekend, a weekend which should rightfully have belonged to Peter except that he had to work overtime and overnight on Friday and Saturday.

"Dan, this is Peter. Peter, Dan." She introduces them, and Peter remains silent and impassive in front of Dan who continues to talk to Lydia alone.

"You might," Dan explains, "wonder what I am doing in a store as chichi and unabashedly fancy as Balducci's, my dear. Aren't you going to ask? Well then, I'll tell you, it was supposed to be a surprise, but if I let you know your appetite will be whetted even further. I am buying wild and fun foods for us, my wild one." By now Peter is alternatively staring at Dan and at Lydia in disbelief but Dan is unperturbed and carries on, "I looked in my refrigerator and told myself next time Lydia will not have to go hungry because she does not like pizza."

Lydia continues to clutch Peter's sleeve; she moves so that her body rests against his, the grey pattern of her jacket fading into the uniform grey of his coat. She watches Dan's face, his moving mouth, the words of seduction rolling from his throat and falling between her and Peter. Dan's eyes are shifting in all directions, fleeing from the select abundance in the store, to the shoppers dressed in *nouveau* Italian clothes, to the salespeople wearing green aprons—yet never resting to acknowledge directly Lydia's or Peter's presence.

"I asked myself, why does she never stay after nine A.M.? She doesn't have a job, after all, and then I said to myself, 'Breakfast breakfast!' That's what it is, it must be breakfast," he looks down into the basket Peter is holding. "Croissants and jam, umm, I forgot the jam, would mustard do? Pure beautiful real yellow American mustard, would it suffice do you think?" And while Lydia yells, "Shut up! Shut up!" al-

41

most everybody in sight freezes and looks at them and Peter
tells her, "I'm getting out of here. You do what you want,"
drops the basket in front of the cashier and walks out of the
store.

*Contents of Dan's refrigerator
after the trip to Balducci's Fine Foods:*

Pizza — very old, curly; one orange slice at bottom
of box it was delivered in; all peppers, mush-
rooms, and mozzarella missing from top
Loaf of whole wheat bread, one end missing
One pound of Danish butter, intact
Jar of honey-sweetened cherry jam, intact
Two bottles of Dos Equis beer
Jar of Grey Poupon mustard

From the desk at his office Peter calls Lydia. He hears her
voice with no high frequencies, the cheap recording of an
answering machine. He hears: "Hi, this is Lydia. I am obviously not here right now but I'd *love* to talk to you. I am so
sure of it, that if you leave me a message I *almost* promise I'll
call you as soon as I am back. Well . . . here comes the beep!"
"Slut, slut!" Peter delivers his message almost screaming in
her machine. "You little slut, you . . ." He slams the receiver
down and cannot forgive Lydia for making him lose his head
and his temper.

Lying on his bed, his hands beneath his head, the receiver cupped between his cheek and shoulder, Dan calls
Lydia. "I am waiting for you," he says to the machine. "The
bread is getting stale, the jam is becoming moldy, and I am
growing old. Lydia, call me call me call me . . ." He does not
leave his name because he knows that Lydia will recognize
him, that she will remember the good times they had together, come back to his apartment and start unbuttoning her
blouse as she rushes through his door.

In the evening Peter sits on his brown leather couch and reads. He never watches TV, firmly convinced it offers nothing that the combination of *The New York Times,* the *Wall Street Journal,* and the *Economist* could not supply. Sometimes the phone rings, but it's his mother, colleagues from the bank, or some old girlfriend whose name he thought he had forgotten. The lemons and the limes in Peter's refrigerator have started to rot.

Lydia sips hot and sour soup sitting in front of Jean-Jacques, her elbows resting on the orange Formica table at Hunan Empire. Jean-Jacques tells Lydia, "You were never so complicated before. Is it you changing or is life really that difficult?" "Don't ask me," Lydia pleads. "Don't make me choose, I don't want to make choices, I don't know, I don't know . . ."

"Will you at least give the man a chance?" asks Jean-Jacques. "Everybody has the right to be stupid at least once in his life, even Peter, perfect though you think he is." He reflects a second and then adds, "Of course, it helps if you're not around at the time he becomes a total dork, but you can never predict the time for sure." "No kidding," Lydia tells him. "I don't know why I even bother hanging around him," Lydia explains to Jean-Jacques.

"Agreed. I wanted to hear you say this, Lydia. To start, he is such a stiff—" Jean-Jacques says, but Lydia is quick to disagree. "No. You don't know him at all, you're wrong. It takes time to discover him."

"It takes time to discover anybody."

"Peter more than most, he is no 'anybody.' He looks like a stiff," she laughs, unexpectedly, "and maybe in some ways he is one . . . in *many* ways actually . . . but he has it all so together. He knows what he wants, what he will do tomorrow and the day after tomorrow and next year. He even knows what is right . . . what he *thinks* is right and what he thinks isn't."

"Like doggie bags."

"Like doggie bags! Exactly! It's absurd and stupid, but at

least he has an opinion about them. How many people do you know who've got opinions? And how many who are consonant to them? Almost zero, right?"

Jean-Jacques looks straight at her, his puzzlement only slightly veiled by the thickness of his circular lenses. "Right," he offers, skeptically.

"Right! And guess what, I know what I get when I am with Peter—and I like it *and* I like him *and* I love him! Okay?"

Jean-Jacques smiles and seconds her, "Okay."

"It's almost kind of true," whispers Lydia from across the table.

Peter calls Lydia and he does not know what to say when she herself answers. He has become accustomed to hearing her low-pitched recording and—at the sound of the tone—replacing the receiver without saying anything. He always assumes Lydia knows it is he who calls even though he leaves no messages.

Keeping silent he hears Lydia's voice sounding at first puzzled and then annoyed, her hellos becoming increasingly interrogative and suspicious. "Whoever you are," Lydia finally declares, "this is not funny." She sounds vulnerable, aggressive. Peter is charmed.

"Lydia? Uh, long time no talk. Well, it's me again, after all, hi. What's been happening?"

"You mean how's Lydia's meat market?" she attacks him.

"I did not call you to fight."

"I'm not fighting . . . I'm only calling it what *you* called it."

"Lydia, don't make it any harder than it already is!" Uncharacteristically, Peter is shouting at her. And then, as if an afterthought, "Did I really say 'meat market'?"

"Uh-huh. Yes. *Oui. Si. Yavol.*"

"Look, Lyd, I didn't—"

"Don't," she warns him, "tell me that you did not mean

it because you did and you know it very well and so do I. And also spare me the apologies, will you?"

Peter breathes deeply. "I did *not* want to say I didn't mean it, I wanted to say ohmigod you don't mean to say I said meat market, oh stupid, stupid me!" he raises the loudness, the pitch of his voice, "Oh dear! how could I ever have said meat market when what I was thinking about was selling melons and trading grapefruits . . . *Your* beautiful melons and grapefruits, Lydia . . . Now, how *utterly* unforgivable of me."

"See you tonight," Lydia interrupts and hangs up on him. At his desk, Peter listens to the humming white noise of the broken connection.

Though the maid has already cleaned up his apartment, Peter walks through it in search of hidden disorder, meticulously observes its flaws, notices the missing corner of one tile in the bathroom, the asymmetry of the paper pads on the desk, straightens the towels in the bathroom, removes his robe from the hat rack and—after carrying it throughout the apartment—brings it back to the hat rack.

Contents of Peter's refrigerator
before Lydia is supposed to arrive:

One lime from the Korean greengrocer
One bottle of Cuervo Especial Tequila, rather empty
One liter bottle of Triple Sec, orange
Several jars of Caviar, one large chunk of Parmigiano Reggiano, jar of Calamata olives, jar of martini olives, jar of cocktail onions
Champagne, Veuve Cliquot, cuvée 1985
Belgian chocolate truffles
Crock of Pommery mustard

When at 8:30 P.M. Peter calls Lydia and asks her, "What's going on? Aren't you coming or what?" she tells him, "I

45

thought you were going to come here. Downtown. I mean, for once you could be the one trekking 'cross the city, right?" "Bitch," Peter hisses while Lydia asks, "So are you coming over or what?"

Contents of Lydia's refrigerator
while Peter is in a taxi heading downtown:

Two cans of Miller Lite
One jar of roasted cashews
Weight Watcher's dinner, defrosting
Four croissants, stale
Jar of English grapefruit marmalade, full
Chunk of cream cheese, hardened and stale
Pepperidge Farm chocolate chunk and macadamia
    cookies
Tab
Champagne, Mumm, cuvée 1986
Crock of Pommery mustard

Sprawled across Lydia's bed, holding a jam jar glass half full of champagne, Peter lazily tells Lydia, "It can't get much better than this." "You sound like a commercial," Lydia says.

In the morning Peter and Lydia share the stale croissants, the flat champagne, and throw away the yellowing cream cheese. "You really eat this?" asks Peter, holding the frozen dinner up in the air. "Darling," Lydia says, "it was defrosting because I never thought you'd come down here. And anyway," she adds, "how do you think I get my looks?"

"So," Peter insists, "now that I'm here may I throw this offensive zero calories shit down the chute?"

"First you get dressed, then you take me to the Four Seasons, and then you can do what you want with all my frozen foods."

"What!" Peter is stunned. "You got more of these?" and

standing naked in front of the open freezer door he finally acknowledges, "Yes, I guess you really do eat this shit after all."

Dan calls Lydia and she answers the phone but hangs up as soon as she hears his voice. He sends her a blank card with "dan" in miniature script on the bottom right corner. She feels sorry for him and cannot forgive his tactless performance at Balducci's, the unhappiness it caused for Peter and for herself.

Peter tells Lydia, "It's hard to accept, but seen from a certain point of view, Dan was not that bad. He was a catalyst, yes, he did tear us apart but now look at me and you— we are more together than we have ever been." Lydia rummages through Peter's refrigerator mumbling, "I could have *sworn* you had some kind of chocolate in here, I'm sure I saw it just last night—" then she interrupts her search and turns to him. Framed by the still open refrigerator behind her, Lydia says to Peter, "You know what your problem is? You always classify people, you thrive on making sure they can't escape the little labels you stick on their foreheads. Dan is a catalyst, Jean-Jacques is a sixtyish romantic intellectual or something . . . and I don't even know what *I* am, what label I've been graced with. Well, Dan is much more than just a catalyst, has been much more than that to me!" "And you really think I didn't know it?" Peter asks her. Lydia bites her lower lip, spins on her heels, and sticks her head back into Peter's refrigerator.

There is no chocolate in Peter's refrigerator. Connoisseurs, it is known, do not keep chocolate in the refrigerator: it loses all flavor at cold temperatures. Because of their high butter content truffles are, however, a different matter.

"You mean to say you've lived a quarter of a lifetime in New York and you've never ordered Chinese food for home delivery?" Lydia asks Peter.

"Well, I don't eat Weight Watcher's frozen pizza either," he says.

Contents of Peter's refrigerator
after the fifth night Lydia has spent at his place:

Nine limes from the Korean greengrocer
Nine lemons from the Korean greengrocer
One bottle of Cuervo Especial Tequila, full
One liter bottle of Triple Sec, orange
Cardboard container of sesame noodles, very spicy
Aluminum container of moo shu pork with straw
    mushrooms, nail mushrooms, and black fungus
    (wood mushrooms)
Aluminum container of General Tseng's Historic
    Chicken, almost intact
Large cardboard container of white rice, very
    sticky
Pepperidge Farm brownie chocolate chip cookies
Diet Pepsi
Several jars of Caviar, one large chunk of Parmi-
    giano Reggiano, jar of Calamata olives, jar of
    martini olives, jar of cocktail onions
Champagne, Dom Perignon, cuvée 1985
Crock of Pommery mustard

"I mean," Lydia tells Jean-Jacques, "I have practically taken over his place and the man does not even mind!" "It's love," comments Jean-Jacques. "It always happens this way. And when you're not there he spends his time contemplating molding Chinese foo yung stuff and thinking about how your lips moved when you ordered it over the phone." "Sincerely? I doubt it," Lydia says.

Peter stands in front of the garbage can, the Historic Chicken in his hand. "We all make mistakes," he tells Lydia, and lets the chicken drop. Peter is generous, continually offers excuses for Lydia's shortcomings, sociocultural explanations for her lack of taste, tender joking remarks on her Long Island habits. "You are worse than Jean-Jacques!" Lydia screams at him. "At least Jean-Jacques is condescending in an honest way. You, if you didn't love me, you'd simply tear me to pieces." "But that's exactly the point! I love you and he doesn't," Peter says.

Peter lets Lydia have the keys to his apartment and does not ask her to return them in the evening when she goes out on her own to see her friends. "You trust me so much?" Lydia asks Peter. "No," Peter says, "I love you so much."

"He insults me even when he does not mean to," Lydia tells Jean-Jacques.

Dan calls Lydia. He hears Lydia's message on her answering machine: "Hi, this is Lydia. I'm not home right now, and in fact I'm not home much these days (giggle). But if you leave me a message I'll get it somehow and I'll call you back soon." He records, "My little wild white slave are you having fun?" Later the same day he calls again and rhymes into the machine, "If you're not having enough fun, remember me, remember old Dan." At Peter's house Lydia listens to her messages with the remote beeper. "Anything interesting?" asks Peter. "A sicko. Twice," Lydia says.

Dan calls Peter's house and Peter answers the phone. "Hi, is Lydia there?" Dan asks, voice uncertain over the phone.

"Who wants her?"

"Any of your business? Look, sorry 'bout that, I'm a friend of hers, O.K.?"

"May I know who's calling?" Peter repeats.

"Dan. How's that? Maybe not the most popular guy in your household right now, but I'd still like to talk with Lydia."

"You're out of your fucking mind!" Peter yells and slams the receiver down. He is glad Lydia is not home yet, then worries about where she is right now.

"Dan called and I told him to fuck off," Peter announces with satisfaction to Lydia. "How *dare* you!" she screams.

At the Four Seasons Lydia eats all the little butter croissants. "It's almost embarrassing," she tells Peter, "but I'm so hungry." "Remarkable and very nice to hear you say that something you do is embarrassing," Peter comments.

"What you really mean is—I am finally learning," Lydia says.

Shyly Peter says, "I have something to ask you," and Lydia laughs, "Yes, I *have* brought my credit card along. I told you to check your wallet before we left home." She calls Peter's apartment "home" by now.

"I have my Amex, don't worry. But I wanted to ask you . . . listen, I don't really know how it's done, it's the first time I ever said this but . . . I would like to ask you if you would . . ."

Lydia stops sipping her cold cucumber soup and stares at Peter, unbelievingly. "*You* want to ask me to marry you?" she asks. Shocked.

"How did you know?"

"Sherlock Holmes. I've never heard you being so muddled up before. And then saying it's the first time and all that . . . I mean, isn't it what they all say?"

"They do?"

"I don't know." She shrugs. "I think so, I mean it would make sense, wouldn't it? You're not going to tell somebody, 'This is only the fifth time but I'm getting better and better at it.' It wouldn't be very flattering, would it?"

"Lydia. For God's sake, this is not at all the way I intended it to be. I mean I did not want to go for a cliché, but it's true, it is the first time I have asked anybody . . . And look, I wanted to say that I love you and if I'm not blind I think you also love me and I don't want to risk losing you again to some moron who'll then call you to pant all over the phone."

"Wait. What you mean is that you are jealous and afraid of Dan, is that it? That you want to marry me so that you can be certain that I won't run away from you anymore?" She turns her attention back to the green soup and pauses as she lifts the spoon to her lips. "Is that how you envision marriage —a lock, a steel chain? Peter, if it comes down to losing and stepping away from each other it's going to happen whether we are married or not . . ."

"I guess I'm a traditionalist at heart," admits Peter. "That's part of the problem," says Lydia.

In her apartment Lydia sits on her couch, a bag of Famous Amos cookies on her lap. She sweeps the crumbs off the upholstery and tells Jean-Jacques, "Sometimes . . . sometimes being in love makes everything so much more difficult. It's not only freedom that is lost. It's parts of you, the parts you have to give up, all the promises you have ever made to yourself and that you won't be able to fulfill if you are two. And knowing that when you eat crackers in bed there will *always* be somebody who complains about the crumbs . . ."

"Come here," Jean-Jacques tells her and hugs her with his long, skinny arms, his fingers reaching for the buttons on the front of her Oxford shirt. Peter's shirt, Lydia thinks, but what difference does it really make? She lets Jean-Jacques undress her, slowly and with many little moans of pleasure. The phone rings and after her message plays she hears Dan's voice asking, "Baby baby baby, when will I ever be forgiven?" "I gotta call Dan sometime," she tells Jean-Jacques as they sit on her bed and he starts to massage her ankle.

Growth

The difference between men and women is that men cannot bleed without hurting and I can, I tell my brother.

Is that what they teach you in school? he asks, and he is obviously amused.

No, of course not, it's my theory, I explain. And, I add, I'm right too, men can't bleed without hurting.

Sure they can, my brother tells me. They can't, I insist, I know they can't. But my brother continues: And if you're gonna go searching for differences, don't you think you could pick more obvious ones? He enumerates: beard, mustache, penis, balls—don't *ever* forget the balls baby—hair all over...

I know about it! I scream back at him. But that's all stuff that's added on, it's like Lego—some of the airplanes are made with extra bricks, so they've got wheels and propellers, and some airplanes don't have them. But the real difference between men and women is what goes on inside, how the body really works.

Testosterone and estrogens, my brother instructs me, but the words mean nothing to me. They don't teach you much in seventh grade, he concludes. He probably learned about the testosterogens at Harvard. I know that at Harvard they will teach you all about biology and hormones even if, like my brother, by the time you have finished high school you have already decided you want to be a lawyer.

They do teach you a lot! I say, but he orders, Stop arguing with me! and walks away. I am lying on the floor and so I simply turn back to reading *Brave New World*. He calls me. Come, he says, get up, I'll show you something.

I take my time and he pulls my arm. Move! he tells me. I'm getting impatient. And although I don't care, he seems angry by now so I get up fast. In twelve years I have learned to protect myself from his rages: the best protection is prevention, don't give him an excuse, just let him see that you sincerely *want* to do what he wants you to do. Avoidance is difficult, I am rarely capable of fleeing: I freeze in front of him and let his anger pour over me, cut me.

You're wrong, he tells me, men don't always hurt when they're bleeding. You'll see, he adds. We walk side by side through the apartment down the hallway to the kitchen and I think oh no, oh no, oh no . . .

In the kitchen he noisily opens the drawers, slams the dishwasher door shut with a bang. I look for the Coke in the refrigerator and find comfort in taking big gulps straight from the bottle: I am a Coke addict, they say, but I make no effort to cut down. Depending on my need Coke excites me, soothes me, gets me high; it's my twelve-year-old drug, my pubescent addiction.

I drink while watching my brother from the corner of my eyes, removing my lips from the bottle only once to burp in silence (I kill the noise by burying my mouth in the crook of my elbow; my brother thinks burps are disgusting).

He holds the grapefruit knife in his hand. I got it! he announces, and I concentrate on the Coke label. I'll show you, he says. Men can bleed without hurting. Come here, he says.

I believe you! I scream. I don't want to see, I believe you, look, I believe you, that's not what I was talking about . . . I plead with him, Don't do it, don't let me see it. I shake all over and repeat, Don't, don't.

There is this thin edge in my brother. Knowing you are scared will encourage him to go further, drive him to play with you until the end, make sure that he can add important pieces and have a lead role in the game. But he can't stand to deal with you when he has gotten you so afraid that your own self has left, disappeared into the tunnel created by fear: because then my brother has nobody to play with and he will start feeling sorry for you. I know safety (my safety, and his safety too) depends on my reaching and entering that tunnel.

I let my voice take over, fill my skull with nonsense sounds. I yell, Don't do it! Put it down! I fling myself at him and say, I was wrong, I was wrong, I know that it's also women who hurt when they bleed, I know about this stuff, put it down, put that knife down, I don't want to see you bleed, not you . . .

My brother puts the grapefruit knife on the counter. He tells me with a sigh, It takes a while to get you to see that you're wrong. I cross my arms in front of my stomach. He says, D'you feel sick? You shouldn't drink that much Coke. He laughs, What've you got, baby, do you have cramps? I do (I really do), but then my brother asks me, Do you have your period yet? and embarrassed but without lying I tell him, No, I don't.

Julia has seen her sister make out with a boy in the back of the car. Actually, it wasn't really a boy, more like a man, Julia says. He must have been at least twenty-five or thirty, she swears. I get goose pimples; Julia's sister is only sixteen, is this what will be expected from me in four years' time, making out with old men in the back seat? The feeling that I have so little time left engulfs me. I haven't learned anything yet in twelve whole years.

I really like your brother, Julia tells me, he's incredibly sexy. God, you're so lucky to live in the same house with him. It is not difficult to imagine my brother and Julia together: the idea frightens me. Everybody is always saying how Julia and I look alike, how we look like sisters. I tell Julia, My brother never gets involved, and she believes me.

I sit in a bar and sip a Coke. I left school at lunchtime and did not get back for afternoon math and gym. There are three guys thumping over a Donkey Kong machine, pushing all buttons simultaneously and repeating "Shiiiiiit" over and over. There is a bartender who is eyeing me, seems suspicious, maybe he fears that I'll sneak rum in my Coke, pass out, and then he'll be held responsible for serving alcohol to minors. There is this guy sitting at a table behind me, he's thin and wearing a grey sweater, and reading *Newsweek* or maybe it's *Time* magazine. I hope my brother won't come into this bar, I know he won't, I am afraid he will. At this hour my brother is working in his office, he rarely takes a break for lunch, and anyway his office is thirty-two blocks away. My brother won't come into this bar and behind me this guy is reading *Time* maybe and has thin shoulders and a thin hollow face; he has Jackson Browne hair and a large grey sweater. I turn around to look at him once more and he stares back at me. There is no way my brother will ever come into this bar. Under the counter I dig my fist and my nails into the folds of my T-shirt. The guy behind me puts his book face down on the table then picks it up, closes it, and places it on the table once again. The Coke is finished and through the straw I suck on empty, a loud, childish noise. He does not let me hide my embarrassment. He says, Would you like another one? and I nod yes. He motions me with his head, come over here. I sit at his table and munch on the ice cubes. I tell myself that

Julia's sister had much older guys and she's only four years older than me.

I always feel a certain tenderness, he says, for women with oversized shirts. When they wear them. They always look small in large shirts, no matter how large *they* really are. And I know there is a mystery in twelve-year-olds, don't you think so too? he says. They are not women yet, not boys anymore, what are they, can you tell me? He arranges the books on a bookshelf, his back turned to me. Can you tell me why you decided to come here, this is not a place for a twelve-year-old (he turns toward me and looks at me and smiles), even for such a precocious one. When I was twelve I never went alone to anybody's home, I was taught not to accept candy from strangers. (He moves toward the couch and sits down.) You were never taught not to accept candy, were you?

I was, I say, I was too. Playing with a book in my hands, not ready to approach the couch, surveying the environment to capture in advance every possibility. This is the first time I have gone to the home of somebody I just met, I say. (I realize having said it was a mistake; he'll think of me as being even younger than he had ever anticipated.) I mean I sort of don't do it often. I like to know what I am getting into before I get into it. *Do* you? he smiles. Yes, it makes everything much safer — you see, I'm sick and tired of teenagers.

He is laughing. You *are?* he asks, You *really* are? Christ, you make me feel old. Now I know what they mean when they say new generations are different. Twelve and already bored with teenagers, for Christ's sake. Let me tell you, I am twenty-seven and I am not bored with them yet, not at all. He stops talking but continues to smile, cueing me that he has just said something very witty. He gets up from the couch. Will you have some wine? he asks. Is red okay?

No thank you, I say. I hate wine. Do you have any Coke? Whatever I say plunges me deeper and deeper into a child's role, and it bothers me that I seem to want to settle in it (but I do hate wine). I drink lots of it. Coke that is.

57

You like Coke? he asks, and I rush to answer, Yes, I like it a lot, it wakes me up and Coke sort of punches your stomach in the morning and slaps your brain and you can feel the bubbles eating your inside. Do you have any Coke? Please?

You are cute, he says. Come into the kitchen with me.

We walk together to the kitchen and he pulls a stool from under the table, says, Sit down, let me look in the fridge. Get a glass, will you?

Which? I ask. Waddyamean, he says. I ask, Which one —sit down or get the glass? He says, For god's sake, don't be an idiot, he says, *get* the fucking glass and *then* sit down, why make things difficult when you don't need to? And he opens the fridge door and asks me, Do you want a beer, and I say, Nooo a *Co*ke, and he says, I can see no Coke, what about a glass of orange juice, and I say, No, don't you have a Coke, and he says, what's *wrong* with you and I say I don't know but I don't know what I am doing here either.

He is sitting on another kitchen stool in front of me. The table is between us. He says, Are you afraid of me? He says, There is nothing to be afraid of. He says, It was a nice bar with nice people, the one where we met, and I am one of those nice people. He says, I never accepted candy from strangers, don't worry, I was always a good boy and I know how to behave with somebody younger than myself. He tells me I can leave when I want to but I don't want to leave now, do I?

C'mon, he says, let me show you my apartment.

May I have some orange juice? I ask.

I see: here is the bathroom and here is the living room with the stereo and the wooden bookshelves with the shelves bent and crooked under the weight of three layers of books. You have so many books. . . . And here is the hallway and the lightbulb on the ceiling has burned out but it looks too high up to be comfortably reached and changed. Here is the bathroom again and all the towels are grey and the seat is up; it's a man's bathroom. Here is the kitchen, Can I have some orange juice, please, I mean if you are *really* sure you have no

58

Coke at all, maybe you can check again in the fridge, I mean one can never tell, there may be some in the back of the fridge or maybe some which is *not* in the fridge. Here is the living room with all your books, but they are stacked on top of each other, so it's hard, it takes time to read their titles. Here is the bathroom and you use Balafre, I don't know how it smells, I know it exists and they sell it and it is supposed to be expensive, but I'm sorry, I don't know how it smells though I can recognize the smell of Aqua Velva. Here is the kitchen and I am sorry you really don't have any Coke at all. Here is the living room and you have all those Rolling Stones records, they're kind of old records, aren't they? Okay, okay, I'm coming . . . here is the bathroom and your shower curtain looks funny. Here is the living room and here is the bathroom and this is the hallway and here is the bathroom and the living room and the hallway and the bathroom. Here is your bedroom.

The mattress is on the floor, that's strange. What I mean is, hey that's neat! But where do you read, I mean, isn't it sort of a bother to have to throw yourself on the floor every time you want to lie down? No, I never saw a mattress on the floor before, at least as a permanent bed. No thank you, I'd really like to go into the living room and check out your books. They looked interesting. Please?

Come here, he says. You are teasing me, he says. Tell me something about being twelve years old, he says. But you were a twelve-year-old yourself, I argue, and walk backwards toward the door of the bedroom. You told me you remember it. He says, I never was a twelve-year-old *girl,* tell me what it's like. I can't, I say, I don't know myself.

I think: I will bleed and I won't hurt. But I cannot tell him this.

I really must go home now, I tell him. It's getting late and my parents are of the worrying kind.

I think: how could I have been so stupid this afternoon, coming with a total stranger to a totally strange apartment, drinking orange juice into which some strange drug has probably been poured and I don't know why I said, Yes thank you, it could be nice, when he said, Want to come to my place for a while? I am afraid but I cannot tell him this.

I know where you live and I will come and see you some other time, I tell him. He steps in front of me. He takes hold of the shoulder of my white T-shirt. What the fuck did you come here for? he barks. He demands to know. He will not let me leave until I give him a decent answer. He is sick and tired of women always using the "I'm afraid" and "I don't know you" arguments to avoid a screw. I know perfectly well what he is talking about. He tells me that I have to stop faking being scared right away or he'll show me something to be scared about. He asks will I stop staring at my shoes and look at him, what kind of fucking game do I play, hanging around in bars and then going into people's apartments? He tells me that if I think crying in front of him is gonna get me anywhere I am damn wrong. Will I look at him? What the fuck do I want? What do I think *he* wants? Will I answer him?

I want to go home, I whisper, and he pushes me toward the front door and he smashes me against it, my back arching to meet the door handle digging into my spine. WHAT? he asks. Repeat what you've just said. I want to go home, I repeat even more softly and I murmur, twelve-year-olds are not the way you think they are.

Thank you, I say as he opens the door. In the street I stand still at the corner, waiting for the strength to lift my arm and hail a cab. Leaning against the brick wall I wait; though cabs are in supply at 4:30 P.M. it takes a long time for my muscles to finally react and obey me. Sitting in the smoke-filled cab I try hard not to breathe. I am shaking all over, but somehow I manage not to get sick till I reach home.

My brother says, I came by your school this afternoon to pick you up and you weren't there.

For a few, long seconds my brain becomes numb and my stomach tightens into a knot. You wanted to pick me up this afternoon? I ask him, and the irony is not lost on me, although it does not strike me as funny then.

Yes, he says, but you weren't there. All your little pink Barbie doll friends were there but you weren't with them.

I was there, I tell him, but I left school before the others did, I did not feel like taking gym. Oh yeah? my brother asks, and I can tell he does not believe me. Yeah, I reply, shrugging my shoulders.

I can tell when you're lying, don't lie to me, he warns.

I'm not lying.

You'd better not, baby. Be careful with me, don't ever lie to me, he says.

I think: I won't lie, I'd really truly better not. My brother was very serious then.

My brother walked into my room without knocking and I was still sleeping and had nothing on and books on the floor and yesterday's jeans on the floor and *Abbey Road* on the floor and my teddy bear in the bed with me.

My brother came into my room and I was sleeping under three blankets and the bedspread was on top of the blankets — it's uncouth, but it was a cold room at night; it was always cold in the winter since I did not like heating and I did not turn on the radiator in my room and did not allow anybody else to turn it on either.

My brother came into my room and I did not hear the door being opened, I was tired, I guess, and he was stepping lightly as he always did because he walked and passed through life smoothly and in a well ironed and starched way, somehow he was so good at ironing life out, he was a master in the art. And there was *A Farewell to Arms* on the floor, and *Brave New World* and *On the Road* on the floor and *Abbey Road* on the floor and my brother came in my room at 7 A.M. and picked up *Abbey Road* and yelled, *WHO GAVE YOU PER-MISSION TO TAKE THIS FROM MY ROOM!* and I jolted up, ninety degree angle in my bed, and was totally awake, my eyes were wide open and my brain could not hold on to

61

any reference point. Clutching a blanket in front of me and pushing my teddy bear under my bedspread to hide him and wanted and could not (but still wanted) to fling my arms in front of my face because I had to react to my brother's fury and a danger I hadn't had time to appraise and nobody can tell how mad your brother can be at seven in the morning when he wakes you screaming and you only want to say, please give me some time, please give me some time.

DID I EVER *ALLOW* YOU TO TAKE *ABBEY ROAD?* he asked and he never had so I kept silent. GET UP! he told me and I couldn't and kept my blanket around my chest and looked at him, registering his order but unable to process and obey it.

GET UP! he told me again, and I said, no, I can't, and the room was very cold and my brother was all dressed up, he already had his polished shoes on and a grey tie with grey soap bubbles on it but he wanted me to get up and of course I couldn't and I asked him please get out of my room but he was holding *Abbey Road* in his hands and wouldn't move.

My brother told me, *get up!* and added, Look, get up, now! Do you think I care about what you're wearing, how you're dressed, or if you're dressed at all? Jesus no! And I could not believe this was happening, especially not at seven in the morning. I got hold of a navy blue blanket that had been hanging lopsided by the side of the bed and armored myself with it, pressed it against the other blankets already in front of me and stared into it and maybe my breath smells bad and maybe I am wearing pajamas after all and maybe I am dreaming and maybe he will leave.

Get up, he says again and he tells me, I don't see the problem, you're still a child, what's the big deal about stepping out of bed if I tell you to? He's my brother, I think I guess, this strange person whom I don't know and can't understand, he's my brother and I can't believe what's happening, that he is telling me that I am a child, that I should step out of bed naked in front of him, that he is mad about *Abbey Road* and then . . . and then *what . . . ?*

He says, I will count up to three and then if you're not up *I'll* get you out out of bed, and he says, One, slowly and he says, Two, slowly and he says, I am counting ... and he says, I'm counting, and he says, I'll give you a second chance —two and a quarter, and he says, two-and-two-quarters-and that's-two-and-a-half, and he says, Twooo-aaannd-aaa-haaalf, and he says, Almost three, and he says, I am warning you, and he is holding *Abbey Road* in his hands and he says, Two and three quarters, and he says, You are smart—you know what comes after two and three quarters, and I yell, GET-OUTOFHERE! GET*OUT*OFHERE! *GETOUTOFHERE!* STOPITSTOPITSTOPIT! and hide under the blankets and hold them tight over my head and cry.

I tell Julia the difference between men and women is that men cannot bleed without hurting. But women bleed more, I add.

Manhattan
Dark and Light—
or The Late-Night Ditty
of Kevin and Emily

Between day and night but after the evening there is a moment of absolute clarity when the edges of water towers are razor sharp and the world is a two-dimensional canvas of black and orange and blue. There are no shadows and there is no depth so brick buildings become made of the same material as the trees near them. Between that moment and the night lie minutes of unfocused numbness when the shapes dissolve their exactitude and only light matters: the white light of apartment windows, the dull glow of orange street lights, the pulsating acuity of planes flying in the darkening blue. And then the sky becomes nothing, wavelength stops meaning color, and life begins in Manhattan.

It was then that Kevin judged it safe to get out of the tub and walk into the living room where Emily—his girlfriend and habitual housemate ever since he enrolled at N.Y.U.—was waiting for him to continue their fight.

"We are out of Mr. Bubble," said Kevin.

"I hope you drank the whole bottle by mistake," she replied with an utter lack of compassion in her voice. Kevin judged it prudent to keep silent for a while.

He was dripping wet on the wooden floor, hoping to impress Emily with an irresistible blend of little boy vulnerability (wet after the evening bath, at high risk of slipping on the floor and breaking a collarbone and a leg, likely to catch a cold and die of pneumonia), and big boy virility, his body glistening and inviting her to join him to discover his prowess once more. It simply wasn't working.

"I think I am getting a cold," he informed her, and Emily stared at him with absolute boredom on her face, rolled her eyes, said, "It's August. No chance," and lit a cigarette, just to annoy him because he did not like her to smoke more than two packs a day.

"Must you?" Kevin asked her, his voice syrupy with concern and compassion.

"What now?"

"Do you really want to smoke? Remember what we talked about last night, about bronchi, black lungs, and our babies . . ."

"As long as I am alive there will *never* be such a thing as 'our babies.'"

"Yes," admitted Kevin, "that's what you also said before."

"I haven't changed my mind yet."

"But they would be sure to have blond hair."

"Blond what?"

"Hair. Like yours and mine."

Emily pushed the stub of her cigarette into the overflowing ashtray and with her right hand blindly searched for the Benson & Hedges pack hidden somewhere in the black couch. Kevin watched her with a hurt imploring gaze, the health of his future progeny fading in front of his eyes.

66

"Please?" he asked.

"I'm sick and fucking tired of this!" screamed Emily, waving the still unlit cigarette in the air. "It's beyond boring —it's sick!"

A puddle had formed around Kevin's feet. He thought that aside from the health risks he was incurring—the deadly combination of wet body, even wetter feet, and exposure to high density cigarette smoke—the water might seep under the wooden tiles and loosen them. In the interests of domestic well-being and preservation he moved away from his spot in the center of the living room and came closer to Emily, attempting to sit near her.

"You're wet!" she warned him, and Kevin promptly jolted his body in an upright position.

"Sorry, I wasn't thinking," he murmured.

"Right," Emily said and stood up. She blew a cloud of chokingly thick and grey smoke on Kevin's astonished face.

"Darling," Kevin said.

"Give me a break."

"It's so . . . unsanitary."

It was then that Emily knew she would leave Kevin for good.

Since Area had closed, night life in New York had not been the same. When the door was nailed shut with green painted wooden boards Emily had suffered as if the nails had been hammered into her very own flesh. Her life had become bitter agony, unmitigated by Kevin's insistence that it would be splendid if they became involved in other, more domestic, activities. Robbed of her territory and dethroned, Emily had not only lost a home: she had lost her individuality, the sense of who she was and of what was the ultimate purpose of her life. She had become an orphan of the city, a homeless of the night.

And now Kevin had decided that he was growing old and bored much too fast, and that procreation was the solution. "I want to be a father before I turn twenty-five," he had announced one morning after making love to Emily. She had shrieked. That and Area's dying: she had recently increased her morning Valiums from 10 to perhaps 20 or 30 mgs, but she still felt very unsure about their effect and about which color was which dosage. Probably her Valium connection— following the lead of the rest of New York—was ripping her off. Giving her 2.5 mgs, telling her they were fives and making her pay as if they were tens. At times she did not even mind it anymore—she was used to the shit that the city liberally and consistently dumped on her. Kevin included.

In the city there is a moment when the opaque darkness of the night turns into light. After its pitch black coming, the night is pierced by searchlights, dazzled by white gases, smothered by orange radiations, illuminated by thousands of car beams and flickering bulbs in bathroom windows. Lying in front of glowing TV sets attractive SJWs and SCMs eat unbuttered microwaved popcorn and watch David Letterman mortify dog owners when their talented pups fail to perform "stupid pet" tricks. On Third Avenue, under the weak light of pure beeswax candles on pink tablecloths, JSWs and SCMs eat goat cheese and basil pizzas, drink chilled white wine, and share guilt about interfaith dating. Under brash Fifth Avenue lights, facing the shadow of Central Park, uniformed doormen walk out of buildings to open the doors of yellow cabs yet never quite make it on time. On the Lower East Side, juvenile hoodlums throw well-aimed stones at neon light bulbs and create minute explosions of sound and darkness on filthy Avenue D sidewalks; drunk, withered bums stand under traffic lights and as the light turns red rush into the middle of the street to rap on car windows, plead, to be refused ten cents; preppies from uptown reassuringly hold their girlfriends' hands on entering dark shooting galleries where they are denied works and junk, where they are robbed of their money including the fare for the cab back home, where their girlfriends' asses are tested and manipulated by unknown filthy hands and they are both too scared to say anything until they get out of the empty building shell and back into the dangerous light. This is the moment when the night loses its dark camouflage to the frequencies of city lights; it is the moment when the night—and all within it—must show its face again. And this was the precise moment in which Kevin smiled at Emily, walked away from her and turned the switch on the wall. Under the sudden light of a 120-watt bulb hidden in a mock hamster cage, Emily observed Kevin's still humid and glistening body and, as in retreat, sat back on the couch.

The lightbulb shape was reflected on Kevin's hairless chest. It formed an almost ideal target, Emily thought, the center of a human dartboard. Looking at him standing with his pleading All-American hazel eyes she thought that if she even spent just as much as one more minute with him, Valium or no Valium she would end up either killing him or killing herself. She picked up a lighter.

"You're going to continue smoking until I don't care anymore and then you'll stop. I'm right, right?" Kevin asked. Mute, Emily started rearranging the black and white pillows that surrounded her. "I think I know what you're doing when you smoke," Kevin continued, "it's your way of telling me that you don't want kids. But you see, somehow I wish you could understand . . . that when people are in love they can tell each other everything. So you can *tell* me you don't want kids, you don't have to smoke it out of your system."

Emily interrupted him, "I've already told you so at least fifty thousand times!"

"Yes. But you don't have to write it down in smoke letters. And also—forget the kids for a moment—when people love each other, they can really tell each other what they want, what they feel and how they are. They *do* tell each other these things but we here, you and even me I'm sure—I mean it's not like I'm saying it's all your fault, that's not *at all* what I mean—but we aren't doing too good a job at it. Not really, I think. And it's really too bad."

"Too bad? That we don't say everything to each other?"

"Well, yes, sort of. That sounds right." Kevin sat next to

her and put his hand on top of hers. Emily edged toward her end of the couch. Kevin stretched his arm to continue to hold on to Emily's hand. "Well, then . . . what are you thinking about?" Kevin asked her.

Emily removed her hand from his. "What?"

"You know . . . like right now you looked like you were thinking about something and it could be something nice so I'd like to share it with you. I'd like you to share it with me, that is."

"This is incredible . . ."

"What's incredible?" Kevin sounded genuinely surprised if not outrightly dense.

" 'Share' with you? Are you from California or something? Jesus, I just can't believe it—"

"Wait," Kevin stopped her, "I'm lost, help me. What's the problem, is it just because I asked you to talk, to share something with me because you love me?"

Emily screamed.

They had been lab partners in "Introduction to Psychology" at N.Y.U. and, though they had both flunked the course, they had made a beautiful pair at Area. The psychology instructor had told them that it was extremely unusual, if not unprecedented, for one student (let alone two) to fail Psychology 101. They had both agreed with the instructor and later that day they had also jointly come to the conclusion that psychology neither was nor ever would be of any use whatsoever in their lives. In the early morning—after dancing, being seen, and doing lines at Area—Emily would walk with Kevin to his mini-loft in Tribeca and watch the sun rise over the mysteries of Brooklyn. This had always been her favorite moment of the day, and before slipping under the sheets where Kevin was already waiting for her, Emily always tried to make sure that the alarm was set for 11 A.M. They had both scheduled mostly afternoon classes but hadn't been totally successful at it.

At Area, Emily had seen Warhol, Christopher Reeve,

and the blond star of *A Room with a View* (though she could not quite remember his name). She had noticed Basquiat and Haring before she even knew who they were but she had recognized them first, and eventually she knew they had noticed her too. Leaning against the bar rail in the back room she had finally introduced herself but had not really been sure they had heard because the music was so loud and her speech maybe a bit slurred. She had told Haring that she loved his style, that it reminded her of children's cartoons and comic strips. One week later her artistic critical ability had been confirmed when she read about Haring's revolutionary cartoonlike figures in *New York* magazine. Proudly she had read the column to Kevin once over the phone and once again that evening, careful to enunciate every word while Kevin mixed gin and lime juice and cut very thick, very straight lines for both of them—their traditional pre-Area tonic.

Patriotically loyal to her night refuge, Emily had attended all significant parties and events at Area. She was not sure of many things in her young life, yet she was absolutely certain of one thing: she would always come to the monthly opening nights at which the club's new theme and decor were unveiled. Dressed in what she loved to call one of her "little dresses"—sequinned-black, tight-and-short affairs from major uptown department stores—she had squealed high-pitched utterances of delight as she discovered the props for the new theme of the month: giant aquariums crawling with spiders and flies, padded transvestites following Jane Fonda's workout, less-than-accomplished actors taking time out from their bartending gigs to iron shirts and watch reruns of "The Honeymooners" behind glass windows.

Emily and Kevin never dared to approach Area's doors before one A.M. By the time they arrived the inevitable pack of hopefuls was already crowding around the club's red ropes. It was a sad, tragic show, definitely worth watching—though only once in a while. While occasionally fun, insistent dwelling on human misery was a trait neither Emily nor Kevin was eager to cultivate. When she was annoyed Emily would sometimes hiss, "Fucking B. & T. assholes," but mostly it was be and let be. The Bridge and Tunnels didn't have much of a chance, especially if they looked New Jersey. "The moron over there," Kevin would point out to Emily, "he is total New Jersey." There was regret in his voice because having to be witness to the basest and most scurrilous manifestations of life pained Kevin deeply. Vacuum packed in a black polyester shirt, black 501s, and black riding boots, the moron made indiscriminately elaborate and frantic gestures toward the doormen. Politely led through the ropes, Kevin and Emily knew that when they would decide to go home and call it a day they would still find him there, waiting and gesticulating and arguing.

One evening somebody had asked Emily if she had ever considered becoming a model. She hadn't thought about it as yet, but it was a good idea. She quit N.Y.U. and heavily invested in partially nondeductible professional supplies. She threw away all the antique Pepperidge Farm cookies and Entenmann's Danish Rings that were growing mold in Kevin's loft, and packed her drawers with Clinique makeup, colored stockings, Dexatrims, and vials containing several grams of blow and guaranteed almost pure speed. Kevin had decided he would at least finish his sophomore year.

"You see," he explained to Emily, "it's too soon for me to decide what I want to do. I just can't say I want to do this or that, I want to be a doctor or a club owner or an advertising man. I can't, not just yet. Or maybe never actually, maybe I will never be able to tell what I will be when I grow up."

"Why do you *have to* decide?"

"I don't know if I have to, but I might. When I was a child all my uncles and my father's friends always asked me what I was going to be when I grew up. I don't know what I told them then, I really don't remember what I wanted to be, but what I remember is that I thought that 'grown up' meant being twenty. Like I believed that once you were twenty you were a real adult who not only knew what he was going to be but who already *was*. And now I am twenty-and-more and I don't even have one clue about the whole mess."

"Neither do I," said Emily, trying to comfort Kevin by sharing his plight.

"Yes, you do, you decided you're gonna be a model. That's *something*."

Emily turned her head slightly to the left, bit her lower lip, and looked at Kevin from the corner of her eye. "Yeah. I guess."

"But I don't have any idea about any of it," Kevin said. "So at this point N.Y.U., even, makes sense in a weird sort-of way — it's something, I go there sometimes. I might even learn something, seriously, if I take it for real."

"You would? I don't think *I* did."

"I don't know. I might, maybe. But I have to do something, I feel it. So then at least for now, I can stick to it and finish the year."

"And then?" asked Emily.

"Then nothing," said Kevin. "Then I might have to decide again. Or we'll decide together, maybe. Like we can maybe move to the Bahamas or Fiji or live in another really amazing place like that."

"Maybe. I don't know . . . I like it the way it is," said Emily.

One night at Area Kevin stopped dancing and said to Emily, "I am tired. Let's go home." Emily gasped and stared at him; when she was sure that he was not making fun of her she started crying. So they had continued to dance, furiously, as if their union, and the well-being of all that mattered and was worth living for in Manhattan, depended on their absolutely and positively being the last ones to leave the club that night.

The next day Emily demanded an explanation from Kevin. She was still under shock though her state was tempered by time's healing effect and by three or four colored Valiums.

"I was really tired, truly and sincerely," Kevin only said.

73

"Maybe you should have done a couple more lines," Emily offered generously.

"Maybe I really was tired, just that once."

"But," she argued, "it's so *not* you . . ."

"I've been going to N.Y.U. very seriously . . . almost," he reminded her.

"Then maybe you oughta give it a break, once in a while."

"What?"

"It's not like the old times anymore," she said, sounding sad and abandoned.

"You're crazy. Nothing's changed at all except that now you just hang around the loft waiting for the Ford Agency to call you and ask you to *please* agree to do some shoots with Scavullo."

It was very true, too true, and it hurt. In orderly succession Emily had thrown at Kevin a plastic ashtray, a garter belt, a pair of red stockings, and a hardbound copy of *Princess Daisy*. Adroitly, Kevin ducked and dodged every projectile but the book. It hit Kevin straight in the stomach, missing by only a few inches his most prized and cherished parts. Aware of his close call with terminal disaster, Kevin collapsed on the leather chair just behind him. Shocked and grieved he avoided looking at Emily. Emily, for her part, did not bother to console him nor try to make his stomach better with loving kisses and therapeutic coos. That night they went to Area but did not make love when they came back home.

Daylight brings punishment in the city summer. Dawn arrives too early; it creeps in before 5 A.M. With its tenuous light it assaults the sensitive, burnt-out eyes of night lizards reentering Manhattan streets after having smoked and snorted and danced in East Village after-hour clubs. Dawn arrives in a muffled, treacherous quiet; it washes littered SoHo streets with buckets of pink and orange translucent color, and tricks tired brains and reddened eyes into believing that the garbage is environmental art, mysteriously planted or sprouted overnight. Dawn lies with breezy promises of a cool, 70 degree day; never still, it twirls deceitful whorls of air along the vertical avenues, approaches couples who wave at invisible cabs on lower Broadway, hugs them and vows that the Manhattan daily furnace is finally over. Dawn is Manhattan's never-never-land, a desert landscape from which all Black, wire-thin bike messengers and plump Chinese bike delivery men have been deported, where empty buses on their solitary journey toward Wall Street have to stop at empty corners to pick up just nobody. In the moment of pre-morning quiet the city suffers, but is never redeemed. Hand in hand, shuffling their feet and legs in the habitual synchrony perfected on the dance floor at Area, Emily told Kevin that she was tired. "Really tired," she admitted, her mouth contorting in an ultimately successful attempt to negate a yawn. Kevin had smiled. Knowingly.

"Do you want to have breakfast someplace?" Emily asked him.

"I thought you were tired," Kevin immediately reminded her. Emily was finally starting to understand his predicament—no, she was actually living it, sharing it with him!—and he was understandably reluctant to let her get off the topic so easily.

"I'm tired *and* I'm hungry," she rebutted, very matter of fact. "Nothing weird about that, is there?"

She was snappy. Poor Emily, thought Kevin, she was obviously exhausted . . . He decided that, given the circumstances and given his love for Emily, he should be especially doting toward her.

He mentally rehearsed a concerned and yet virile tone of voice and asked, "How about getting croissants at the Koreans? We can bring them home and warm them up in the oven."

If Emily was impressed with Kevin's display of domestic know-how and familiarity with major appliances, she was careful not to let it show. "The Koreans?" she had thrown back at him.

"Yes. The deli. We could pick up some croissants and . . . oh, some melon too, let's say."

"I was thinking about breakfast *some*where . . ." she said, pleadingly.

She is whining, thought Kevin, and then immediately began to work hard at erasing the wicked thought from his mind. Yet—though he lovingly watched poor, weary, and hungry Emily shuffling her tired feet alongside him—he could not help admitting to himself that Emily was, indeed, whining. He felt irritated by his own lack of devotion, and became silently angry at Emily's persistent, slightly atonal, requests for food and rest. He looked at her trying to find a cue to help him decide what to do and how to feel.

"Kevin. Honey. . ." said Emily.

He fell in love with her once again.

After a short discussion they decided to have breakfast at the Empire Diner, and ordered apple pie and a Bloody Mary for Emily, steak and eggs and a Diet Coke for Kevin. At dawn they could go anywhere they pleased: breakfast was free territory, the time in which Emily and Kevin would finally become independent after the night's obligations. The real alliances were those of the night.

"I am also kind of worn out," Kevin confessed to Emily.

"'Also'?"

"Yes. Like you, right? Didn't you say you were tired before?"

"Tired, *not* worn out. It's very different. It only means that what I need is one day's sleep, not sleeping therapy."

"I didn't say anything about sleeping therapy," and suddenly, seized by an impulse he could not well identify nor understand, Kevin challenged her: "Tonight I'm not going out. Maybe I'm getting old, I'm really sorry, but I just can't hack it."

Emily did not even look at him. She finished slurping the Bloody Mary, thrust her arm up in the air and called, "Check!" to the waiter dozing behind the counter.

For the first time, that morning there was a brief but

76

painful period of estrangement between Kevin and Emily. That night at 1 A.M. Emily stepped out of a cab and — resolute and alone — was allowed through the red ropes and welcomed into her club.

The break in his nightly routine allowed Kevin to concentrate on his N.Y.U. classes. He finally discovered what they were about and dropped out before his sophomore year was over.

"I mean, I had to think hard about what it was all for and realized that there was no way that all those classes were going to help me make any kind of decision about what I'll do later on. So then, really, what's the point?" Kevin asked Emily.

"Precisely," Emily said.

"And now we can be together again," Kevin promised her. Emily smiled, reached across the coffee table, and pulled a small lacquer box toward her.

"A line to celebrate!" Kevin announced.

"Lines, honey, lines," she corrected him.

During the day Kevin and Emily slept, made love, lay down to think, and tried to decide what color they should paint the bathroom. Kevin also wrote minimalist contemporary poetry and Emily worked out in deference to her budding modeling career. They both watched "Wheel of Fortune" and "Jeopardy" and thus acquired much useful knowledge in the late afternoon.

When the Palladium opened its gates their mailbox was deluged by garish invitations. Sorting through the offensive orange and yellow cards Emily said to Kevin, "Seems like good taste is a thing of the past."

"Why don't you just junk them all, then?"

"Too easy. I mean, it's kind of cool to check how low they can get with this stuff. At least Area has fantasy, what they send out is real. But look at this" — she lifted a piece of crimson cardboard in the air — "ten dollars before eleven P.M. to hear some rapping band. I mean, who the fuck do they think we are, New Jersey or something?"

Kevin wholeheartedly agreed. In light of the esthetic turpitude that the Palladium inflicted upon them both, Emily and Kevin decided that they would never bother with it, never grace it with their presence. Five days later, piqued by irresistible curiosity though tormented by shame, they handed their passes to the Palladium's doorman and walked into the club's amplified cacophony.

Later that night, before going to sleep, Kevin told Emily, "There might be some room for repentance in our lives."

Emily didn't say anything. She was concentrating on the painstaking task of removing her makeup without removing any facial skin cells. Skimming her cheeks with a cotton puff she completed her motions before she finally deigned to answer.

"Huh?"

"Repentance. You know."

"No."

"Yeah. I thought so . . ." Kevin pondered the difficulties involved in setting up a philosophical exchange with Emily before trying again. "Like—don't you feel sometimes that something is missing?"

"Like what?"

"Uh, I don't know, like faith and believing. Some kind of purpose, that's what I want to say!" Having found just the right words he felt triumphant.

"Not really." She had turned her face away from the mirror and was looking at him. Kevin was lying belly up on the bed, his exposed face betraying his confusion. "Why? Do you?" she inquired.

"Me what?"

"Have a purpose and all that jazz . . ."

"No! That's exactly the problem! And maybe we've done it all wrong, and we're doing it even wronger now and we should sort of repent and ask ourselves what it's all about. Like—the Palladium, we both thought it was totally out and gross and Jersey. But then you look at it for real, be open about it, and is it really *that* very different from the rest? Area and all, I mean."

Pained, Emily looked at Kevin and told him what she had never dared say to him before. "Go to sleep," she whispered and then, quite ashamed of what she had just said, she mumbled, "You make me say things I don't even believe in," and busied herself by looking for stray Valiums in her jewelry case.

Mercifully, when he woke up that afternoon, Kevin seemed to have already forgotten the morning's despair. He held Emily tenderly under the shower, tolerated her using his "Clinique for Men" shampoo, lied to her twice by swearing that she had both lost weight and developed very well-defined and yet undeniably feminine deltoids, and finally suggested that they spend a very domestic evening together before going to Area. " 'Domestic?' " asked Emily. She had difficulties fitting the term in her vocabulary, it was so completely alien to her own life-style.

"Yes. You and me, here. We can order sushi and sashimi or something kind of raw like that, and then sit around and watch 'Miami Vice.' We've never done it before . . . Could be fun, I mean it might be worth a try, just for the experience."

Emily contemplated what Kevin had just said, considered the dreadful implications of expressions such as domestic, home-delivery, and watching TV on Friday night. She was beginning to feel more than slightly hysterical. Kevin emerged from the kitchen area eating a Granny Smith apple and wearing only a pair of boxer shorts embellished by miniature pink and blue whales. In his right hand he held an Oriental-looking menu.

"California roll?" he asked.

"Which is what?" sighed Emily.

Kevin was taking a long time to check through the take-out menu. "Cucumber and some sort of fish, I think," he finally announced.

"Kill me . . ." sighed Emily.

"Chinese, then?" he proposed.

Almost analytically, Emily watched Kevin as he studied the Chinese menu. He wanted Chinese noodles, he wanted the two of them lying on the couch, he wanted "Miami Vice" on a Friday night: Emily simply did not.

In view of her impending modeling career, of the dubious origin of the food (who had ever heard of Foo Chow Imperial Restaurant?), and of an unspoken—and yet very real and rather hostile—statement directed at Kevin, Emily refused to eat any of the Chinese food he placed on the coffee table. Yet it was all very pretty, and Kevin was looking perfectly at ease, perfectly *domestic,* as he piled rice and beef on his plate and then drenched it with the contents of all five pouches of soy sauce.

Kevin then insisted that they watch "Miami Vice." Between 9 and 10 P.M., Kevin repeatedly commented on Don Johnson's well-publicized sex appeal, remarked on Don's hairless chest, and finally spent a considerable amount of time—including all commercial breaks and every chase scene lacking presence of weapons—commenting about his own rather hairless chest, his quite hairless legs, and his not-too-short blond hair.

At 10 P.M. Kevin pressed the "OFF" button on the remote control, and, turning his attention to Emily, he addressed her directly. "Quite something, huh?"

"This? You mean, like, one hour of two cops modeling for *GQ* and on top of it one is black and the other is basically bald except for the top of his head—"

"You didn't like it?"

Emily opted for honesty. "I fucking hated it! And what I hated most of all were your stupid comments and the smell of that Chinese beef something sitting in front of me for the past two hundred hours."

"Sometimes," Kevin was almost hissing, "I think that you don't even have an inch of an idea of what you want but it's O.K. by you because whatever I do is wrong anyway."

"You think too much," Emily said.

When they finally started on their pilgrimage to Area,

Emily and Kevin were not on speaking terms. That night Emily busied herself by standing in front of the bathroom, waiting in line for her turn to cut lines on one of the club's strategically buffed and well-polished toilet seat covers. Kevin, sipping large quantities of gin and tonic at the bar, was finally noticed by a considerably more mature woman who usually spent her nights playing supporting roles in off-off-Broadway experimental plays, drank some more gin and tonic with her, was dragged to the ballroom floor and made to follow her graceless motions as Prince's "Kiss" hammered into his ear canals, and kissed her as they both waited for one last drink at the bar. Kevin followed her home and the cab kidnapped him all the way uptown, stopping only to land him in front of a pre-war building next to Columbia University. A stranger in a foreign land, scared, guilty, and reminiscing about the many joys he had shared with Emily, Kevin lay perfectly still throughout the night. Horizontal on the futon, he resisted the actress's attempts at oedipal seduction, and got only a stunted reaction when she removed his belt and pants. Disgusted, she kicked him out of her apartment before 6 A.M.

In the taxi Kevin promised himself that this would never happen again, renewed his love and commitment for Emily, and asked the driver to stop at a curb so he could run into a 24-hour store and buy a dozen assorted roses and carnations for his beloved.

Emily was asleep when Kevin tiptoed into his apartment. He placed the flowers in the sink, lay down near Emily, and fell into a deep, effortless sleep. In the late morning Emily confessed to him, "I was so out of it this morning that I didn't even look for you when I got back. I just dropped dead on the bed. I mean, I just wanted to sleep . . ." Kevin, understanding, magnanimous, nodded and Emily accepted his forgiveness.

They still loved each other . . . or at least, they were sure they did. Without exaggerated recrimination they removed each other's strands of hair from the bottom of the bathtub, would throw away the Sunday comics section without arguing about who had read it last. They would continue to execute their beautifully choreographed entrances into Area (but not into the Palladium, of course), to perform their synchronous dancing, and—at the very fringe of the night—seek mutual warmth by huddling one against the other under the top sheet, always one-hundred-percent cotton yet much too light in the chilly Manhattan August nights.

Even in the middle of the New York summer there is a moment of the night when all becomes chilled and still. Sometimes the chill just lasts a brief instant, for only a glimpse of the summer's ephemerality; sometimes the cold lasts minutes and even hours, lingers long enough for lone sleeping people to awaken, pick up the bedspread from the foot of the bed and wrap it around their bodies, long enough for sleeping lovers to move closer to each other and find physical comfort in their joint protest against the season's treachery. Sometimes the cold arrives but does not leave: it remains, stable throughout the night, to indicate what the morning will be like. Then late-night owls must roll down their shirt sleeves and prowl through the city in search of diners or after-hour clubs without air conditioning, the luckiest prostitutes are allowed to flee their street corner and wait while their pimp books them a hotel room, newspaper boys and garbage men and Hong Kong traders mutter *"hijo de puta"* and "jesus-fuckingchrist" as they walk rubbing their hands together, and the trees in Central Park drop unexpected leaves on the hardened ground. Generally, in August, the cold of the night does not last very long. In August Kevin and Emily did not have many occasions to huddle against each other under the top sheet.

Sitting on the bed Emily asked Kevin, "Are you coming?" and tortuously slid her legs into black lacy stockings.

"Where to?" Kevin said; he turned his head away from Late Night's stupid pet tricks, and looked at Emily. "Mmm . . ." he added. Emily thought that by now Kevin's skin bore the imprint of evening upon evening of stupid pet tricks shows.

"Guess."

"Mmm . . ." repeated Kevin.

"Out."

"Area?"

"Yes! Surprise!" Emily mocked him, and Kevin sharply turned his head back to face the set. "Stupid pet tricks!" screamed Emily, making it sound as much an insult as she possibly could, making Kevin feel as if he were part of the stupid pet tricks himself.

"Area!" he replied loudly but lacking the enthusiasm of Emily's delivery.

"So, are you coming out? It's up to you."

She had finished squeezing her minimal hips into the stockings and was searching in the drug box for some early evening coke. Kevin alternated between looking at her and at the screen. He watched Emily unscrew the cap of the glass vial, drop some powder on a mirror, and cut herself a line. She had not even offered to cut one for him. "You go ahead," Kevin told her.

That night Emily came home early. Her nose and her eyes were red, and black mascara stripes drew grooves along her face. She sniffled and—unmindful of the price tag of her little black dress—she wiped her nose, her tears, and her mascara on the black velvet of the left sleeve.

Kevin was sleeping when she walked through the door. He finally stirred when she began to sniffle louder. He stirred and she sniffled; he turned and she sighed; he burrowed his face into the pillow and she whimpered; he complained " 'milyyy . . ." and she started to cry audibly, sobbing and heaving. Kevin finally lifted his head and opened his eyes to confront her pain. Devastated, she was standing still in front of his bed, tears streaming out of puffy eyes.

"They've closed it . . ." she wailed and then again, louder this time she repeated, "they've closed it! It's over!"

"Say what?"

"It's boarded all over. And yesterday it was so alive, it really was."

"Emily? What's over?"

"Area. I got there and there wasn't even anybody to tell you what happened, it was *horrible,* they just killed it from one day to the next and we never knew it was coming and we might have done something to keep it open . . ."

He was the man, he had to be in charge. He tried to reassure her: "Emily, they must just have had everybody sick on the same evening. Like the bartenders and deejay and the ropers—"

"No," she flung herself on the bed next to Kevin and he wrapped his arm around her frail shoulders. "It's really totally over. You could tell."

"Poor baby," said Kevin caressing her hair. Emily's tears left blots of black liquid on the sheets.

Had they been more diligent about attending Area they might have helped prevent its downfall. Had they brought more friends along they might have persuaded whoever was responsible for Area's closing that he needn't fear about the club's popularity. They missed its crowded intimacy, the music that over the years had progressed from funk to disco, their success over the natural selection conducted in front of the red ropes. Emily pined for sights of Haring and Reeve and Warhol, for meaning and purpose. Kevin regretted all his missed possibilities and longed for the recognition that now belonged to the past.

They chose stupid pet tricks over the Palladium. Ultimately, watching the show had led Kevin to want children.

"They would *not* be 'fun,' " Emily argued.

"It'd be something else," Kevin would explain, frustrated by her inability to empathize.

"That's not enough—surely."

"That's a lot. And it would mean something."

"You've got no idea what you're talking about," Emily rebutted.

"Sure I do," he argued not very forcefully.

"You've never even *seen* children!" she tried to reason. Kevin sat on the couch waiting for David Letterman's announcement that new pet tricks would be revealed in that night's show. "Lassie. Tommy, you know, Lassie's kid," he replied absentmindedly. David Letterman appeared on the screen and proclaimed that a Doberman would perform next. "Stupid *owners'* pet tricks!" said Emily with anger. Emily, Kevin sadly thought, had not yet recovered from the loss of Area; he, on the other hand—being the psychologically stronger of the two—had been able to manage the stress much more efficiently. For yet one more time he puzzled about the possible reasons for which, despite his keen psychological insights, he could have failed Psychology 101.

He resolved to trust these insights . . . have Emily melt with desire at the sight of him, perceive him as the man she had always wanted, know him as the bearer of the seed of the child she did not yet know she wanted. He stood up, started to unbutton his jeans, and told Emily, "I'm taking a bath. Care to join me?"

"I'd rather watch the stupid Doberman!" she told him and, as Kevin walked into the bathroom she yelled after him, "We're out of Mr. Bubble!" loud, yet not enough for him to hear.

Lies and Babies— at Twenty-Nine

We knew it would be a lie from the time we started. My mother is much too old to understand but she still said, "You don't know what you're getting into, better let him go before you get so hurt you come to cry on my shoulder." At twenty-nine I'm almost thirty. At twenty-nine I don't cry on anybody's shoulder anymore: I haven't cried in six years and, all of twenty-nine, I look at him shaving under the shower and I'm embarrassed by his stomach, the ingrown hair on his chin, my unshaven and stubbly legs.

I stay up at night. Nothing can put Charles in a good mood before eleven in the morning, so I go to sleep late and I wake up late and then sometimes it all works out beautifully. Very very rarely, though, and lately, never. Things have been tough here in Salinas (little work which makes for no money and no fun just plenty of boredom) and especially tough between Charles and me.

I leave some toothpaste in my mouth in the morning and in the evening. I avoid rinsing my mouth well because I like the red gel taste. When he remembers to brush, Charles is painfully careful. He refuses to view my not rinsing as a choice. "It's carelessness," he says, "you go through life as a slob and expect people to clean up."

I don't want his water, I don't want his judgment, lately it's been getting worse and worse, lately it's been him and me arguing about how much toothpaste is left in my mouth, lately it's been Charles telling me, "I ain't gonna look after you," and then saying, "Go rinse your mouth, you're a slob in the morning."

I'm no slob in the morning. I shit and piss and brush my teeth and choose not to rinse, all of which is more than what can be said about Charles. Enough said already, anyway.

A fireplace and snow and real hot chocolate with some raw egg yolk in it to make it even thicker and Charles asked me if I wanted some Wild Turkey in the cup and I thought it was a terrible idea—why spoil good, real, almost velvety hot chocolate with alcohol?—but I said yes, please, and the taste almost made me gag but not Charles, not him. Charles coasted from the kitchen, heating more milk and cocoa and chocolate in the pot and back to the table to add the Wild Turkey and then to me waiting in front of the fireplace and us just talking, nothing but him telling me about California and Oregon. Talking till we had both drunk our cups and he'd be back in the kitchen for more, stirring the wooden spoon in the pan, passing the egg yolk through a sieve to make sure no egg lumps would find their way into the cocoa. He seduced me with chocolate and milk and Wild Turkey. Only the Wild Turkey and Jim Beam are left now.

My mother's house is in the Los Gatos hills and, day after day, she has nothing to do but move from kitchen to bedroom to living room and back to the kitchen again, think about me, call me, and complain. Sometimes she sends me magazine clippings with recipes, especially those for "Meals for a Whole Family for Less Than Five Dollars." My mother says: "You're young enough to build yourself a respectable life with a respectable man. I don't like to give advice but I don't want to see you come to me crying and telling me 'you told me so.' Because you know, I'll answer 'yes, I did tell you so.' " I'll never let my mother say to me: "I told you so," though she's dying to say it.

Charles has a child with a woman I've never seen, his ex-wife. I have never seen the child either, though I am the one who picks her birthday and Christmas presents—Barbie dolls and Barbie outfits mostly and always. I know the child is five or seven (can't remember exactly and it does not matter anyway) so Barbie dolls are just right.

Once I had this idea during the night and, startled, nudged and woke up Charles and asked, "Charles, how old is Andrea?" I had this image of a seventeen-year-old girl surrounded by pink Barbie dolls, but then Charles answered, "Now . . . ? What fucking difference does it make?" He was right, especially at five in the morning and so I went back to sleep and I kept sending Barbie dolls.

Charles's ex-wife has been calling him a lot lately so now he doesn't want to answer the phone in case it's her on the line so it's either been me answering or the phone has rung on empty for full minutes at a time while we yell at each other, "Can't you get that thing off the hook!" She calls him and if I answer she screams from Pittsburgh, "Tell that bastard that the check is six months overdue and we can't eat Barbie dolls for dinner!" She screams, "You slut, what's he giving you, steak dinners so that he can make sure he's got enough money to let us starve?" She screams, "Tell him we're getting a *real* lawyer now, and he won't be able to sit on his big fat ass no more."

At first I didn't tell Charles about the calls but nowadays I report each and every one of them to him as they arrive. I say, "Charles, she called again to tell you you're an asshole," living my anger through her phone calls. Lately I haven't minded answering the phone so much after all.

The problem is that Charles is feeling himself turning into an old boozer and I see it just the same but I'm really scared only for myself and not for the both of us. Four years ago, when he'd cook stew with red wine in the evening, when I'd come home with fresh zucchini and a half gallon of ice cream wrapped in newspaper to keep it cool, I cared and worried for us both. I'd pour red wine in tall blue Mexican glasses, at the table I'd agree with him that his ex-wife was an asshole, and we'd chew the meat slowly and pick the sauce up from the plates and the pan with Italian bread. Charles and I both brushed our teeth after dinner before making love, although we would sometimes forget.

Now there are times when Charles does not brush for days, his teeth become first opaque and then yellowy, his breath heavy with the rotting; he does not brush his hair and it falls on his shoulders and stays there, curly black strands— almost pubic—on his grey sweatshirt; he does not shave and the ingrown hair digs further into his cheeks and chin forming red and black and white bumps, mountain geography underneath the beard stubs. When Charles finally shaves, the cut bumps become holes for a colander of blood and I hear him curse in the bathroom, emerging with a Bic razor in one hand, holding a towel to his face with the other. By now, all of our towels are dotted with brownish blood marks.

My mother says: "At twenty-nine you should be able to live in a house with clean towels. Is that too much to ask from life?" No, I won't let her know how much I long for pink suburbia towels: some people even get their initials embroidered on them. If I weren't almost afraid of Charles's reaction I'd buy "His" and "Hers" towels and tell him to stick to his.

"If I still had my job," Charles says, "I wouldn't have to get bored over a bottle."

"If you still had your job," I tell him, "you'd be getting drunk over a bottle at the bar. At least now you're staying home." I know I'm being unfair but I don't care.

"You're a bitch! From one bitch to another, is that what I've earned in life? Whaddya want me home for *anyway?*"

"Not much, you're right—you haven't fucking earned anything in one whole year!"

"Shut up!" he screams. "I'm warning you!" And I pay no attention to his warnings. He sits at the kitchen table, his stubbly chin in his hands and screams. He's too much of a vegetable to even bother to move.

When Charles had a job he'd be away from home for days on end riding his truck from Salinas to Ohio and back again. I don't know about all he did and screwed on the road and never asked, asking is not my style. And, anyway, he never brought back any veedee, he'd just bring me *National Enquirer*s and *Good Housekeeping*s he picked up on the road, and coin machine combs and, sometimes, a menu stolen from a truck stop. I hung the menus on the kitchen walls and they became a record of all the places he'd been to till one day he and I got into another fight and I tore them off the walls. We didn't bother to stick them up again even after we made up.

Charles had this trucking job when I met him, when I moved in with him and waited in Salinas for him to come home. While I waited I read, cleaned up in the yard, picked up debris and disgusting weeds, rotting peels which had failed to become a compost pile. I cut fabric into dress patterns but never got around to sewing them together so I finally took a box of pieces of sleeves, fronts, and backs to the Salinas Salvation Army, sure that their volunteers would get into a frenzy at the sight of all that sewing to do. I had Junior College skills in typing and bookkeeping, but there was no typing or bookkeeping to be done around Salinas, just lettuce and avocados to be grown and shipped. So while I waited I bought cuts of beef at the wholesale market and chopped them up so that, when Charles came home, he'd have everything ready to start cooking. I read every *Reader's Digest* I could get my hands on (they are less fun but more interesting than *National Enquirer*s) and whenever I got to the "Life in these United States" section I would imagine Charles and me sending our contribution, winning the three hundred dollars, and buying ourselves matching couches and a loveseat. I clipped recipes from Thursday's papers and got bored and more bored so that, by the time Charles came home, there'd be one or two empty bottles of Jim Beam on the kitchen table and he'd curse at me for being a drunkard.

"Okay," I said, "I'll stop drinking but you stay here with me."

"I'm not staying anywhere, and you don't start blackmailing me, you hear?"

"I'm not blackmailing anybody, I'm just telling you how things stand. You're away, fine, you've gotta travel, you've gotta travel but then I've got the right to choose what I want to do while I'm home."

"Not fucking finish a Jim Beam bottle in just two days, no you don't."

"Like you never drink on the road?"

"Like I *never* drink on the road, that's right!" And by this point we would be shouting at the top of our lungs.

Lately my mother's been saying; "Tell him it's over, you haven't even married him yet. It's not like you're his wife or something and gotta stick to him for the rest of your life." My mother is Catholic and believes in eternal marriage and eternal divine punishment in case of divorce. Somehow, though, my having lived with Charles for four years does not bother her much. For her it's better living in unmarried sin than living a divorce. I'm not going back to my mother, I'm not going back to any yellow house with a woman that wants me there so that she can talk and criticize without pause.

Lately Charles's ex-wife called and said, "Tell him I'm giving him two more weeks and then I'll ship him his bastard kid and every fucking Barbie doll. I've got it all counted up, he owes us more than a thousand dollars, you hear? And the kid doesn't even know her father but she soon will if he doesn't pay up. Tell that bastard—" I slammed the phone back on the hook because I couldn't stand her yelling anymore. Actually, it wasn't only her yelling; rather, after slamming the phone down, I realized that it was her insulting and cursing Charles so much that bothered me and I thought, hmm, maybe I still feel for Charles more than I thought and expected. I wanted to shut her up by punching her mouth and though I don't consider Charles my property, no way, he is still much more mine than he ever was or is hers: at least once Charles and I loved each other and nipped at each other's ears and licked each other's chests with true delight.

"What'd she want?" asked Charles back in the kitchen.

"She says you either pay her a thousand or she's sending you the kid."

Charles started laughing hard—more like a wild loud grin, actually.

"She's sending us the kid?"

"She's sending *you* the kid."

"It's *us*, honee, you always wanted a baby, didn't you?"

No, I've never wanted a baby. In this I differ from other Salinas women, my friends, who beg their boyfriends to marry them fast so that they can get pregnant without feeling the guilt of a husbandless motherhood. I remember myself as a child—constantly whiny, learning late (very late) to be toilet trained, mouth and hands sticky with lollipops and Crackerjack caramel, breaking dishes I was supposed to wash at the kitchen sink, cutting my dolls' hair to see if it would grow faster, howling as my mother braided my hair in too tight pigtails, hoping for years to be kissed and touched by a boy before I even knew what I really wanted and what it was supposed to feel like (good), hiding everything I could (cigarettes, dope, diaries, beer, myself) from everybody and from my mother especially, cutting classes to hang around in total boredom, telling my mother she did not understand me even before we both became aware that was true. I think of babies burping and babies shitting and boxes of clean Pampers and garbage pails of soiled Pampers, acid milk and green baby gag, endless never-coming burps, a collection of relatives coming in to goo-goo and ga-ga over the baby's crib, colics

93

and crying that never stops when you wake up at night torn between the real impulse of smothering the kid under the pillow and the civilized response of picking it up in your arms whispering, "Shhh, shhh." I think of baby talk and never saying, "Horse, dog, train, stop it!" but "horsy, doggy, choo choo, and no no," of spending hours kissing invisible bumps and cuts to make them better, mashed and strained food and the endless bulk of semi-empty baby food glass jars in the refrigerator (mocking with their "no-salt" and "no-sugar" labels the neighboring six-packs), and before that the formula tins opened and closed and mixed day after day, boiled bottles with rubber nipples left to dry all over the house, and even before that my breasts leaking through my bra and in bed at night, my own nipples cracking and oozing milk and blood maybe so that I can be the baby's milk farm and I say no, no thanks, I do not need a child now, I do not need to marry to feel complete and whole.

"You know damn well I don't want a child around," I said to Charles.

"You got a choice, honee," he mocked me. "D'you got one grand?"

That's how Andrea arrived at our doorstep with a small red plastic backpack on her slim shoulders and carrying two large A&P shopping bags full of Barbie dolls and Barbie clothing, one bag in each hand.

The child knows we don't want her. Better yet, she knows nobody is really begging to have her around. She's just slightly thin (promise of a coltlike teenager that will emerge soon) with chipped blonde hair, green eyes, and the look of somebody in a waiting room, of somebody who wants to let you know that she's hanging around only for a moment just till she can or has to catch the next train. She's nine and looks seven at times, at times she looks eleven and I wonder if she's already got her period or if I'm supposed to tell her about it before she gets scared out of her wits and thinks she's dying of cancer the way I did when I was eleven. But then again she's really Charles's daughter and he should be the one to handle this kind of crap. *If,* that is, the kid is his daughter.

"Look," Charles says the evening she arrives, Andrea exhausted by the Greyhound trip across half of the States already asleep on the living room couch, "I'm dark-haired and her fuckin' mother ain't no blonde either so can you tell me how this kid can be mine?"

"You recognized her, didn't you?"

"I didn't recognize nothing, her mother tells me one day that I got her pregnant and now I'm a father and better marry her—"

"Yes, I know."

"So what was I supposed to do, tell her she was a liar? For all I knew at the time it could have been me."

"And maybe it was."

"Goddam *no!*" he shouts and slams the Bud on the table, some warm beer sloshing out of the can. "Look at her, does she look like me? I've been tricked for nine fuckin' years, now it's time to call her up and say you keep the kid and I keep the dough and just to do the kid a favor she can keep all the Barbie whatchamacallits that she cares to keep and that's it. An' I don't wanna hear 'bout no bastard kid of mine ever again, hear? That's what we gotta tell her."

Charles's shouting woke Andrea up and, still lying on the couch, she is watching us through the open kitchen door. Her eyes are sleepy but wide open, as if stoned. She mouths something and I get up, go next to her and ask, "What?"

"Where's the . . . bathroom . . . ?" the kid whispers and I realize that we have both forgotten to show it to her or to ask her if she needed to go after her journey. Poor kid, I think, maybe she's been dying to take a piss for the past five hours and all the time she was too shy to ask. So I show her where the toilet is but then I think she could have asked anyway, couldn't she? No nine-year-old should ever be so stupid, I think, and don't feel guilty anymore.

My mother says: "What kind of man is a man who won't recognize his kid when she's in his own home?" It's useless to

95

explain to my mother that it's not his kid, she wouldn't understand. She says: "What's he mean it's not his kid? He sends a kid birthday presents for ten years and then he's got the guts to tell her, 'Excuse me kid, but it was all a mistake'? Don't tell me you can call this a man." Sometimes I wish Andrea had curly black hair and brown eyes, it would all have been much simpler.

Andrea stayed with us for five whole days. She sat on the living room floor and played with four Barbie dolls (all called, with a dazzling lack of imagination, Barbie: Barbie-one, Barbie-two, Barbie-three and four) moving her lips as if forming words and speaking, though what she was saying I couldn't tell since her voice never rose to more than a hissing whisper. On the third day, looking at her, I remembered I had forgotten to send her a Ken. "Come with me," I told her, and we took the bus to the shopping center.

She seemed amazed by it, strange, since the shopping center was nothing but a dozen old stores around a parking lot and the kid had been raised in Pittsburgh, a real town to which Salinas is no match at all. Still, she looked around like she had never been in a place with so many stores and things in them; when we walked into Woolworth's she even seemed afraid of touching anything—as if the greeting cards and the colored pencils and Crayolas, Mister Clean and mops were all waiting to bite her if she came too close.

"Here," I told her when we reached the toys aisle, and handed her a box with a Ken in it, "your Barbies need a man."

She was serious and beaming at the same time. Don't know how the darn kid could *do* it but she could, she wasn't smiling or nothing just holding the Ken box in her arms with this un-fucking-believable look on her face, like a woman who's just had a child, I guess, and is exhausted and already wondering about all the Pampers and formula but, all the while, she's just ecstatic and she'll never let her baby go or give it to anybody, wants him in her arms and on her stomach forever.

That look in a nine-year-old almost killed me. I became the wild one and rushed up and down the aisle and got the kid a box of Crayolas, sixty-four, all sixty-four of them including the built-in sharpener, and a pair of butterfly combs to put in her stringy yellow hair, and a coloring book with Barbie and Ken and friends on the cover. Almost twenty dollars to the wind, and all for a kid nobody wanted.

Charles and I screamed at each other that night. Charles has no job and has taken to drinking more and more just on its own—that is, for no reason associated with food such as before dinner or during lunch or while eating chips in front of the TV—and me, I've got a lot of lousy part-part-part-time jobs that bring in no money, and Charles couldn't understand how I could have spent all of twenty dollars almost to buy stuff for a kid who wasn't even his.

But he hadn't seen the kid's look when I handed her the Ken box, or he would have done the same, just the same as I.

Charles and I woke up the kid with our screaming and it didn't bother our fight a bit. He yelled that I was worse than the kid's mother, that I was just out to suck money from him.

"It's *my* goddam money!" I yelled at him. "Can't you remember who's been earning 'round this house lately?"

"Shut up!" he says, defeated because I am so right. "Shut your trap up! I didn't ask them to give me the sack—"

"I didn't ask you to have your kid come 'n' stay here. I didn't ask you to stop sending money to her mother either, did I?"

"She's not my fucking kid!"

"You tell that to her mother."

"You . . ." he chokes, unable to go on, crushed it seems by the rage which has grown and swollen in him since he's stopped driving from Salinas to Ohio and back again. He rests his head over his crossed arms on the table. I feel pity and a new love for him, and it lasts until he lifts his head and I see his face, the unshaven beard stubble and him crushing the Bud can with his hand.

"The kid has to go," says Charles and, although I wish I could fight with him, on this point I have to agree.

"Yep, the kid *has to* go," I repeat back to him.

We called the bitch back in Pittsburgh and though she did not seem overjoyed to have Andrea return she did not seem too displeased either. I guess she had developed some kind of habit for the kid and it had been harder than expected to break free from it.

Andrea left on the bus and since I did not know what kind of sandwiches she liked I was careful to give her every kind—ham and swiss, bologna, peanut butter and jelly. It was when I was patting the bread slices together that I noticed I had no idea of what the kid had eaten during her stay in Salinas, that I did not know what she liked or wanted and that, really, I had no notion of what she was like. It didn't matter, it was a bit late anyway, but the thought got me somewhat sad. I mean, the only thing I knew about her was how she didn't seem to belong to us or anywhere, that she liked Barbies and Ken and that when she colored in the coloring book she did it very slowly and carefully, never smearing Crayolas out of the picture outlines. Guess it's really not much to know about a kid but, deep down, I must have known she wasn't with us to stay and so I never bothered to learn or notice more. It would have been wasted energy anyway.

My mother screams: "You let that poor kid go back to her mother?" pronouncing mother as if in a spit. "D'you two got no heart, are you made of stone? That mother didn't *want* her and you still send the child back?" Now, my mother has never even seen Andrea, but it's just like her to become the protector of small creatures as long as it does not affect her personally. She hates thinking about killing moles and foxes but if a mole started digging in her vegetable patch or if a fox killed her miniature dogs she'd be the first one to take the clubs out and go hunting, hungry for a killing.

So my mother asks, "How could you let the child leave?" and I say to her, "Mother, we did not let her leave. We *shipped* her back. Charles and I don't want children around just now, and Charles is in no mood to have to babysit for a child who is not even his."

"How does he know?"

"*We* know."

"You can't tell just by looks; you need a blood test, I tell you, he can't just say it ain't his child and that's it."

"Mother, enough said 'bout this, okay?"

"No, not enough said," she protests, too taken by the gossip that Andrea's existence, arrival, and departure have provided her. "Looks don't tell the whole story."

"You didn't even get to see the child!"

"Five days, five days, I ask you, how was I supposed to know she'd be leaving the same week she arrived . . ."

"I had told you the kid wouldn't be staying long—" But my mother does not want to listen to me anymore, she just wants to talk and talk and let me hear all of her outrage and righteousness.

"Five days, had I known I would have run to see the child, let her know there was at least one person who wanted to make her feel welcome in California."

"We made her feel welcome." We both know I'm lying.

"How?"

"Mother, I'm geting tired of this talk," I tell her and my mother mutters about the kind of daughter she has. My mother never liked Charles, and from the beginning she believed our living together was all a lie (a lie of and about love and trust). She was right but it isn't my style to let her know about it.

The kid gone, Charles asks me, "Do you want a baby now?" and I'm furious with him. I tell him he's ridiculous, I'm not having no kid from nobody especially from a man who'll then tell me the kid is not his.

Charles shaves under the shower and tells me, "You're still young enough to have a dozen kids if you get down to it right now." I throw a grey towel (dotted with brown dry blood specks) at him and the flow of water from the shower head interrupts the towel's path so that it does not hit Charles; it falls, wet and limp, at the bottom of the tub. "Okay then, so you're young enough to have ten kids," compromises Charles.

"I *could* see you with a big belly," Charles says in bed and he takes his own pillow and snatches mine from under my head, places both over my flat stomach. "Wait," he orders, and picks a robe from the floor, slips the belt from its hooks and ties the two pillows on me. "Get up," Charles says and pulls me up, wraps the robe around me and tells me, "Keep it closed, c'mon honee." The robe is tight around me and I spin on my heels and toes around Charles and Charles turns around the room and watches me. "Mmm, my little Madonna," he teases. "Ever heard of hysterical pregnancies?" I ask, and he's rolling on the floor — literally rolling on the floor — convulsed with laughter and soon I'm rolling too, on the floor and over him with my robe still on but open and the two pillows still tied to my stomach though they've moved sideways toward my hips, and with the pillows in between we play and make love, we have to invent new rules for our game, the pillows slide up and down but me and Charles make sure the belt is tight enough so that, protected by the pillows we can have fun and make love, make love and not just fuck like other nights. He says, "Oooh, my sweet Madonna," I tell him, "I got twins just for you," he bites into the top pillow and says, "I'm eating your child up," he bites into the bottom pillow and says, "Beware I don't bite your guts out," he bites into my breast and I cry, "Ouch!" and from across the pillows I slap his shoulders while he licks me and furrows with his head in between the pillows moaning with pleasure.

Charles sits at the kitchen table scratching his head and the pimples left fresh on his skin since he's shaved this morning. Flakes, tiny flakes of dandruff fall on the folds of fat on his stomach. He scratches his pink hairy belly and the dandruff settles there, among the hair.

"D'you ever think about Andrea?" he asks lazily.

"No," I lie.

"Neither do I," he lies back.

"Do you want a child?" he asks, still scratching.

I look at him scratching and drinking and a wave of disgust overcomes me and I think this man wants a child, he wants a family and a wife to be the mother of his children, he wants children and Pampers and Disney Time on TV, he wants a son to drink Buds with when he's fifty and the son is twelve, and a daughter to dress all in pink, and I tell him, "No. I want to leave."

"Whaddya mean?"

"I don't want no child of yours. I don't even know what I'm doing here with you."

"You're burning the fucking toast!" he screams, and I remove the charred bread from the broiler and throw the slices on the kitchen table; they land in front of him, one slice slides all the way down to his lap and burns his naked hairy stomach. Charles cries out in real pain and anger, "You bitch! You fucking bitch!"

"You make your own toast!" I scream at him and run out of the kitchen and into the bathroom, listening to his yelling, the oven door banging, the repeated "You bitch" reaching me from under the door crack and through the wood. I think, I am all of twenty-nine and I feel like one hundred. I think I know twenty-nine is close to thirty but I never knew thirty could be so bad.

I sit on the can and put my head in my hands and I'm so sad, my head so heavy and full with tears and hatred and booze that I don't even have the energy to get it all together, to get out of this house and into the car, to press my foot wildly on the gas pedal and call him from Berkeley to tell him to send my things—all my things—ASAP.

My mother says: "When you're ready to move out on him you can always come back here, your room is waiting for you. I won't even say 'I told you so' when you come back, though you sure deserve it." What would I do in a room with pony posters, Nancy Drew books, and old moldy-smelling Barbie dolls? I could send the dolls to Andrea, that's what I could do, send her the posters and the books for when she's older so she won't need to tread in the Pittsburgh snow to get to the public library. Sad to think the only person who'd like what I own is Charles's bastard daughter. The kid we sent away on the Greyhound bus after just five days.

"You didn't give her a chance! You didn't fuckin' give her a chance!" I yell at Charles from inside the bathroom, the locked door a shield between us, and I start screaming, the anger of Andrea voiced through me now, and her pain is sobbed through me and after six dry years I break down and cry out and weep at Charles, "You never gave her a chance!" tear at myself, "*We* never gave her a chance!" I hear the alarmed voice of Charles from behind the door, he's never heard me crying before and sounds stunned and afraid. Sitting on the can I cry and cry, reach for the handy toilet paper roll to blow my nose, remain locked in while Charles tries to coax me to leave the room.

"We didn't give *who* a chance?" he wants to know, but saying "Andrea" would sound too weird and almost stupid so I just rock myself to calm for hours of seemingly endless tears which stop as the toilet paper roll nears the end.

Charles hugs me when I walk out of the bathroom and I notice that a six-pack is out of the refrigerator and on the kitchen table, certainly Charles's welcome back gift after my afternoon exile.

We celebrate my return with boilermakers, playing at creating the perfect bourbon patterns when the shot glass is dropped into the beer mug.

"If I get pregnant I won't be able to drink as much," I say to Charles.

"Don't worry, babe, you ain't gonna get pregnant, we'll both be careful," he promises.

"What if . . . ?"

"What if what? And then what? And maybe?" Charles teases me. He places his thick strong index finger against my cheek and slides it down following the rim of my nose. "You done crying for the decade," he announces, and I look around the kitchen and there are cigarette butts in the ashtray on the table and Jim Beam and Bud cans on the counter and on the table and a puddle of defrosted ice near the refrigerator. There is a pan with cold canned beef hash near the sink, it's been there for two days and we don't know whether we should eat that shit before it turns green or just plain throw it away, there is a 1984 calendar on the wall we never removed because Charles likes the picture and I tell Charles, "Yes, I'm done crying," and feel myself dry up inside again.

A Way with Words

As I moved from truth to meaning, from meaning to words, and from words to sounds, there was only one more way to go: from sounds to silence. I don't know if silence is the solution. I know, however, that I cannot any more impose on Christopher the voice that defines me and the lies that I carry in my voice, that I cannot be witness to my own falsehood. If my love is only words, then it is no love at all.

Christopher always wants to know if he is the one I love, if he is the only one, if I love only him. In the first weeks I myself believed in my answer. "I love you, only you, more than anybody else," I would promise him and wait for him to hug me and make love to me. But one day we were walking toward the subway and he asked, "Do you love me?" and as usual I reassured him, "Yes and yes and more than anybody else," at which point he started arguing with me.

"If you love me more than anybody else, then you love lots of others too."

"My parents," I said lamely. I am thirty-one. Too old, we both knew, to think about my parents when I think about love. Christopher is just seven years older than I am, and I am not sure what he thinks when he thinks about love.

"You know that's not what I mean."

"What do you mean then? That you are so emotionally immature that you cannot even stand the idea that I love somebody else even just a little bit? Must it be you and you and only you all the time?"

"Yes!" he yelled, and precipitously crossed the street before the light had turned to green.

Christopher has not stopped asking me if I still love him, if I love only him, if I love him as much as he loves me. How can I ever know how much he loves me? How much reassurance does a thirty-eight-year-old man need? I don't need it, I sure don't need reassurance with words, but Christopher does, day in and day out. I have learned that Christopher clings to my words, sucks on them for nourishment and life. My words are love, for Christopher. So now I lie to him every day, day in and day out. Like in the past I tell him, "I love you, only you, and more than you ever thought I could love you and more than you know." Christopher does not ask for more and I am happy to give him my lies as a gift. Words, lies, cost so little after all.

This is years ago: the TV was showing an old Marlon Brando movie in which he played some sort of war hero, wounded and paralyzed yet still looking as virile as ever; leave it to Brando to be able to pull such tricks, I thought, and then remarked to my mother, "I've never seen a really sexy paraplegic yet."

"Did you ever try LSD?" she asked me, and I thought, "What???" and did not know what to answer. On the screen Brando continued to grin from his wheelchair and my mind was filled with psychedelic Day-Glo paisley, the battered cover of *The Electric Kool-Aid Acid Test,* my days at Stanford, the smell of rancid bong water and gingerbread burning in the oven (we did not have the strength to detach ourselves from our stoned slumber and remove the cake), the endless minutes becoming visual hours while I struggled to walk up the stairs to my apartment. "Do you really want to know?" I asked my mother.

"I guess you're right . . ." she said and let the matter drop.

What I had really wanted to ask her was, "Why do you want to know?" But, instead, I had decided to shelter my mother and myself. Growing up means knowing when to shut up. It means knowing when to lie, when to tell the truth, when to decide what to say rather than just saying it. Even my own self-awareness, the consciousness of myself, is filtered through my words.

Lying in bed, my hands crossed beneath my head, my elbows sticking out as if in defense, I asked my lover, "Do you have any children?"

"Now, do you really think I want to answer a question like that at such a moment?" he answered, and I imagined the charring pins of guilt plunging arrowlike through him, his necessity of denial as he lay naked, his thigh touching mine, in my bed. "No," I said, "you probably don't."

Christopher would cry if he knew he is not the only one. What I will never be able to explain to him though, is that he *is* the only one. I don't consider him to be my "lover"—he is more than that, our relationship much more complex than the simple word "lover" conveys. My lovers are ephemeral, they come and they go, and they choose to make love to me or to fuck me in between. Christopher is no lover, my lovers are not like he is: I do not pick lovers who cry, who need to be comforted with words, who request incessant confirmation of love. I pick lovers who prefer action to words, who show me with their bodies and not with their minds, who don't question but demand. Christopher is the man in my life, the only one. But this, even as hung up on words as he is, he would not understand. So I never tell him much and he does not know me.

When I was a child I could never understand if you were supposed to tell on somebody or not. Children's rules dictated that no, you obviously weren't supposed to, and if you did (if you reported to the teacher that Johnny was copying your spelling quiz or that Jane had written on her desk the dates for the history test) you were a creep, you were a moron and a leech and nobody wanted to play with you at recess.

But adults' rules were less absolute, so much more elastic and complex that I could never make sense of them and master them. They said, "Don't be a tattletale," they said, "If I wanted to know something about Johnny I would have asked him myself," they said, "I can see for myself, thank you," not meaning the "thank you" at all, of course. But they also said, "If you knew he was copying, why didn't you let me know?" and, "You know that she was not supposed to go in the street alone, so why didn't you run to tell me?" and, "If you know about something wrong and you don't tell me about it you are making yourself partner in the crime."

I never resolved the dilemma, the first incertitude of my immature moral philosophy. I still don't know when I ought to tell and when I oughtn't. The responsibilities of my speech and of my silence overwhelm me. I did not know what the "musts" of my teachers were, I don't know what the "musts" of my being with Christopher are. What I must tell him and what I should never let him know. Ultimately, he loves me because I have somehow struck the right balance, my words are right, what I say is appropriate. My words are the dress with which Christopher clothes me.

I said to Christopher, "All teenagers have secrets that they are too ashamed to tell, even to their friends."

"You too?" asked Christopher.

"What do you mean—me too?"

"Did you have secrets?"

"Of course!" I laughed. "I said 'all' teenagers had them. But I don't even remember what mine were."

"How unnecessary...you bitch!" hissed Christopher. Not meanly but he meant it, still. He felt threatened because I had hinted at the possibility of not telling him something. I thought about his response and wondered which of us was the smarter one, me with my forgotten secrets or him with his need for their denial. I am smarter, he is smarter...I was reluctant to come up with an answer because I hate to come in second. I especially hate being the judge and arbitrator of my own defeat, having to acknowledge that Christopher has a point, that I have hurt him, that I might lose him if I am not careful about what I say.

I went with Christopher to Alfred's party. Christopher was rather reluctant to join me because Alfred was a friend from my side. Christopher claims that he does not fit in well with my crowd: what he really means is that he feels neglected when I cannot give him my absolute, undivided attention. But then, as he always does, he came along because—crowd or no crowd—he would rather be with me than without me. Personally, I do not particularly care one way or the other.

I have never been to a party where there isn't at least one person trying to impress the others with his skills. Pouring beer or freshly opened Coke in a glass without making any foam; drawing very straight and yet not too narrow cocaine lines on a mirror with only a normal kitchen knife (you get points if the knife is serrated); winning at Trivial Pursuit by answering every question correctly, even the ones which— through an impossible and tortuous misrepresentation of se-miotic rules—require you to distinguish between England, Britain, and the United Kingdom. I listen to their chatter, the noise of people deeply satisfied with themselves and with their own achievements, and I wonder, "Don't they have any modesty, weren't they ever taught that you don't brag?" But they look so happy, so content, and the beer really does not form a head when they pour it. They are insufferable and yet—like old aunts who provide a whole month's worth of gossip within the span of an afternoon's tea—they also lend life to the party: because of them shyer people are led into trying to emulate the foamless pouring, drawn to share tales of perfect white lines they have experienced or created, suddenly remember the name of Lucille Ball's baby. Because and thanks to them I can disappear in a party and not feel it is my duty to entertain the anonymous crowd around me.

And there I was at one of Alfred's parties sipping my fifth o.j. and rum, hearing Christopher's omnipresent chatter, feeling out of touch with everything that was happening around me and longing to be back home, still in time to watch "Saturday Night Live." Feeling that nobody but Alfred and Christopher knew who I was, and in fact nobody else did; feeling that I could very well have dropped dead or fallen asleep in one of the bedrooms and nobody but Christopher (who knew me too well to matter at the moment) would have noticed anything special or remarked on my absence. Scary and frightening, an abyss of non-Self, of non-Ego rendered more acute by the numbness of the rum. My life (*our* lives, I should say) are a struggle to create an image for ourselves and then hope that people will notice us, that they will recognize our image and impress it—indelible and significant—on their minds. Being in a situation where our image has no importance whatsoever, where our "I" has no outline or color, robs us of our very own selves: alone we do not suffice to maintain alive the form that our self-representation should take. Crowds scare me not because of their size or because of their anonymity: they scare me because of *my* very own anonymity within them.

So at Alfred's party, having experienced my very evanescence, I had to help myself remember me. Remember who Elizabeth was, my name, my I, my Ego, my Self. Christopher was looking at me and I did not care to let him become aware of how dispensable I was, of how much I did not exist if I did not talk. I had a feeling of urgency, there seemed to be so little time . . .

I looked around, careful to avert Christopher's gaze. Somebody (an anybody, really, just as I was an anybody and a nobody to him) was busy artfully hand-rolling three European-style joints, narrow at the bottom and large at the tip, a skill that any Europe-bound traveler is likely to acquire in Italy or France. I approached him and asked, "May I give you a hand?" and settled near him without waiting for his answer, reached for the dope and for the Bambú papers and rolled this beauty, two papers wide by two long by two across at the tip, the whole thing filled with the best Hawaiian, a killer.

"Care to light?" I asked my neighbor who was still holding his unlit European-style but wimpy joint in his hand. A small but interested and probably knowledgeable crowd had congregated around us waiting for the Communion to begin and for my smoky Host to be passed around and settle on their avid lips.

"Wheredyalearn?" said a Rasta-looking man, asking the question as though he were uttering a unique monosyllabic word.

"France and Italy and England. Europe," I answered only somewhat laconically, secretly glad he had asked, waiting for more questions from the crowd. But nothing further came, all I had gotten for my effort was the Rasta's utterance and a few tokes from one of the best and most beautiful looking joints ever. Mine. The guy sitting next to me, always holding his pitiful abortion of a joint, got to talk with everybody, and I learned he had just painted three black canvases, that he expected to get into a group show in the fall, and that his name was Marc with a *c* and not a *k*. Nobody asked my name, at Alfred's party, and still nobody but Alfred and Christopher knew my name when I decided to leave (much too late to catch "Saturday Night Live").

I had been a nobody for three hours straight. Me, my Self, the whole image I have so carefully crafted since my beginning, for almost thirty years, had not been accounted for, had been worthless and had eventually disappeared: neither joints nor drinks had been able to rescue it.

I needed Christopher, his recognition which—like a deity's breath on a golem—would fill me with life and substance. I needed somebody to tell me (through words, through caring) that I existed. I turned to face Christopher but just in time I recalled that he was not what I needed. What he wanted was to be loved: he did not want and did not care to recognize me, he did not love the me that existed beyond the words I spoke to him. Nice words, loving words. "You are my one and only. I love you more than anything and anybody, I will love you here-and-now and there-and-then and everywhere-and-anytime." My speech and lies are my gift of love for Christopher: they are me. The two are interchangeable for Christopher.

I am at a loss as to what to say, my words (truths and lies, it's all the same) betray me. Beyond Christopher, all along the tortuous path where almost as milestones stand the men of my life, I continually have to face the insoluble choice: whether to betray myself with the truth or to betray the other with my falsehood.

Jordan is a name always, a place almost. Jordan asked me, "What would you like for dinner? I'll make anything, I'll cook everything for you, I'm here just waiting for your orders." He looked comical, a too-tight apron barely covering his naked chest and his blue jogging shorts, so willing to please me: almost too much so. I wasn't hungry at three in the morning and—at that very moment—I loved Jordan, whom I had met that very evening. "I'm not hungry," I told him. "Suit yourself," he said and took the apron off, walked out of my kitchen and into my bedroom. I followed him there, expecting him to be waiting for me in bed, ready to throw myself over him. He was pulling his jeans over his shorts. He left and I never met him again, but I really hadn't been hungry that night in my kitchen at 3 A.M. I shouldn't have told him so. A mistake. *My* mistake.

I told Martin, "Martin, I love you." I thought, "He obviously knows I am saying it because it's midnight and he smells and tastes like no other man I have ever kissed smelled and tasted before. He obviously knows that I cannot *love* him this midnight, when we have only known each other for two intermittent days." It was not even a lie, it was simply a distorted truth, a truth that depended for its existence only on us— Martin and me—being together at that moment. It was a truth that would be a lie a minute later and that would have been a lie a minute before. It was a truth but it became a lie as Martin did not recognize my intentions.

Martin said I had misled him all along. "All along?" I argued. "I never did! I never told you I loved you . . ."

"Oh yes, you did," said Martin, and he was right. But only insofar as he was concerned: me, on my part, I had never told him I loved him. And if I ever had, the taste of our frantic kisses at midnight should have been enough to let him know what I really meant.

I tell Christopher that I want him near me forever and for always. I lie.

I call him from work and whisper in the phone, "Do you miss me? Are you thinking about me now? Don't answer, just tell me you do." I do not leave him a choice, to direct him to what he must say, I whisper, "I miss you too," before he can answer. I lie.

Christopher is not lying when he tells me that he wants my love for him never to end, that he needs me, that he cannot live without me. At least, I don't think he is lying. I hope he isn't. How can I ever, really, tell?

I need the logic of grammar to comfort me when language has become my traitor. If speech cannot communicate who I really am, if it carries lies as comfortably as it carries truths, then I want the unpolluted, absolute order that transcends the words themselves.

Christopher tells me that I am stuck on grammar. That grammatical mistakes are not really mistakes but simply ways by which people make their lives easier, by which they communicate without the burden of constantly stopping to check their language.

"Speaking is communication," he argues. "It is not an art, but you make it into an art. You are like a sculptor, chiseling away to reach perfection, and in the meantime you demand either silence or perfection, nothing else. You won't accept anything in between. It's unreasonable!"

But it is not unreasonable. Already his words and my words lie. Now he wants me to believe that it does not matter if the very system on which words rest is polluted: that chaos is acceptable.

Words have no substance, no truth. They lie and mislead us; naked and robbed of meaning they play nonsense games in my brain, scramble my connections to the people I know and love. To the people and objects I think (presume to) know and love. Myself scrambled, I even lack the words to understand the vacuum.

Christopher mops the kitchen floor. He uses Spic 'n' Span, Mop 'n' Glo. I won't mop the floor until I can deal with the cleaner's name, until I can accept that its sound and its meaning and its construction are correct and congruent. I am not evading responsibility, it is not laziness on my part. I cook, make the bed, fold my and Christopher's shirts, but I won't mop. In the supermarket Christopher dragged me to the household cleaners aisle and told me, "Pick a name you like, anything, any name." How can you choose a name when you don't know what it's really supposed to be?

"I cannot tell what is right," I said and pushed the cart away, toward the end of the aisle.

"Why don't you just acknowledge you don't like to clean floors?" Christopher asked.

He did not understand, he really did not understand anything at all. Explanations were useless so I told him, "I love you," and before he had a chance to argue, "What does it have to do with cleaning floors and Spic 'n' Span?" I hugged him from behind, I pinched his ass and said, "I like to see your ass when you are bending." It was all the explanation he needed. He seeks comfort in the signs of my love.

But I cannot give signs anymore, I cannot separate myself from my words, and my words don't sound real. Their sound is not my sound, I don't recognize myself in it. I don't know, I cannot tell.

The sound of words should be the sound of speech, the sound of what we want to say to each other, but it isn't. Sound does not determine what I say to Christopher: it hides the meaning of my lies, transforms the meaning of my truths. Christopher will never be able to know what I think of him, and I will never be able to hear him and understand. Sound covers our messages.

I want to find the words and cannot do it anymore. I cannot say, I cannot talk, I cannot lie. I enter the microscopic world of sounds, of words which, stripped of meaning, remain auditory skeletons in a communicative void.

"I will get you a present," Christopher promises in the morning. I nod.

"What do you want?" he asks, but I cannot tell him. My mind is blank, I cannot see what I want, let alone tell him. "A surprise?" he suggests and I smile. "Give a hint," he says and I want to scream and plead, "Words, give me words!" but instead I blurt out "Cat!" "Cat" is an easy, direct word. It is so simple it almost sounds right, it says what it means. Christopher looks at me, intrigued.

"You want a cat?" he says.

"No," I tell him, "it was a voice exercise."

"You are weird and I love you," he tells me before leaving. "Love—lovelovelovelooove," I think as he walks out the door.

Alfred called me and asked through the unnatural, inhuman distance of the telephone lines if I would like to come to a party two Saturdays from now. I heard his voice and the words he said and even understood their meaning. But, all the while, I was unable to convince myself that it was really Alfred talking, even though it sounded like him. The words slightly drawn at the end ("partieee," "Saturdaeee"), the almost breathless and chopped excitement with which he had greeted me as I picked up the phone ("Elizabeth! Liz! Darling! Howya' doing! Listen! You busy next Sat? No, no! I mean two Saturdaeees from now"), the Midwestern nasality that smoothed the possible hard edges of his speech. The words he had uttered were Alfred's typical words, starting with "darling" and with the "howya' doing" which betrayed his true origins; even the meaning, the two-Saturdays-from-now party with lots of coke and booze, had properly seemed to belong to Alfred.

But there was the distance, the unanswered suspicion that there really was no speaker at the other end of the line, that it was all a joke or a lie, that the words I had heard had been generated by an extraordinary linguistic apparatus capable of producing a perfect rendition of Alfred's own talk. Still holding the red phone receiver in my hand, in the absence of any visual cue, I came to believe that there existed no phone line at all but only a strange red machine—which periodically disturbed me with an imperious ring.

"Are you coming then?" asked Alfred, "Say, are you there? Can you hear me? Can you hear me? Darling, is anything wrong, can you talk? Hey, wait, there's something wrong, I can tell, can you talk at all, are you still on the line? Christ, don't play these games with me . . ." His voice (*the* voice) droned on and on, in a crescendo of nasality and staccatos; as time passed the voice became increasingly hectic and

I silently listened to it with growing attention and intensity, catching its every nuance, the changes in tonality, the variations in pitch, and the descents and ascents of its loudness. And then, with an almost categorical change, the voice completely ceased to be Alfred's. That's when I placed the receiver back on its hook and sat on my bed to listen to Albinoni's "Adagio Veneziano" on my CD. No voices, no noises, no staccato sounds, only the mellifluous melody of violins, the ineffable, soothing sadness of strings.

"Did anybody call?" Christopher asked.
"Nobody-somebody," I answered.
"Nobody *who?*"
"A voice," I said.
Christopher came close, and stared at me. He did not know what to make of me and I did not know what to make of myself either. I heard him ask me, "Are you okay? Are you—" but I ran away from him before I'd be forced to hear more and be made aware of how he saw me without my words and my love for him. Once in the bedroom his sounds mixed with the white noise of the air; I threw myself on the bed and, for safety's sake, piled one pillow on top of the other and buried my head underneath.

I look at "Miami Vice" and the Armani jackets disintegrate, the aqua couches and swimming pools evaporate. Sonny and Rico and the pink flamingos disappear in a foggy haze, in the multicolored pointillist reality of a cheap TV screen. I hear the cocaine-driven music of the show and I am able to follow everything perfectly, everything up to and including the last final shooting and Sonny's two hands clumsily wrapped around his gun. I do not even need to hear the shots to know that they—whoever "they" are—are dead.

"Dead," I tell Christopher. Christopher is by now used to my verbal reactions, my "idiosyncrasies" as he calls them. He thinks of them as linguistic or maybe even only verbal or phonetic idiosyncrasies, not as pieces of my Self, of my voice, that I choose to offer him.

"How would you know?" he challenges me. "You weren't even looking at the screen. And, by the way, does anything interest you anymore these days?"

I find the strength of my old voice to lie once again just for him, "Yes, you." And pulled by its power of deception, by the lack of truth demanded by the words and by the sounds, I find the strength to continue the lie. "You and only you and forever you and more than anything and anybody you," I promise. I see that Christopher is smiling but I do not even need to look at him to know it anymore.

In their confusion words engender my horror, carry my fear. I run away from Christopher, his lips his love his voice his breath. The sounds, the sounds... The night train from Boston to New York and the clanging sound of the iron and steel carriages rattling on the iron and steel rails: trying to fall asleep but feeling utterly incapable of doing so, unable to perform an action as simply animal as sleeping. The arhythmical furious sound of the running train keeps me awake, the auditory proof of motion terrifies me, leaves me clutching the arms of my seat until my knuckles become white and my hands have lost the strength of their grip. Motion isn't space, motion isn't sight or fast passing time: motion is sound. I cannot escape it even when I run away. At home, I know, Christopher is waiting.

When there are no more words left, when sound is everything but is so much, so enormous, that it cannot represent anything anymore, then silence is the only alternative: the silence of one's own voice and the silencing of other people's voices.

Lying in bed, his sweaty hand resting on my stomach, my lover whispers to me, "I might have a family but you are my only love now." I do not even stop to wonder if it is the truth, if it is a lie, if it is the truth of the moment... I almost do not hear him but it is not only because he has spoken softly. When he whispers again, his words noiselessly tumble on the pillow between us and silence envelops me like a shroud, smothers me in a wordless cocoon, smothers me in the seduction of its womb.

Three Very Good Friends, and Accessories

Pierre and Mary and Tom have known each other for a long time, ten years give or take a couple of months to be exact. They lived in the same dorm in their senior year in college ("University," Mary clarifies), in the same one-bedroom apartment in New York just after graduation. They had shared everything then, seven years ago, everything, that is, except Pierre's expensive organic vitamins. Pierre has not bought organic vitamins with a pesticide-free guarantee sworn on the label for more than five years. Looking at him, Tom sighs and says, "Maybe you oughta start taking those vitamins again."

"I'm okay, don't worry about me," says Pierre and coughs. He has narrow shoulders, and even his chest has remained as narrow as it always was—if not almost narrower. Pierre's slenderness prevents him from looking seriously like a grown man: when he wears his jacket and tie he resembles a tall fifteen-year-old clumsily playing at being his father. Women often love this, and he loves to acknowledge the tenderness that he provokes in them.

Tom remembers aloud, "We shared everything, even the Ma Bell bills, even the cat food and cat litter bills, even—"

Mary cuts in, "You guys never shared *me*, don't get it wrong. I was the one who had it doubly good, it's the truth. What we did share," she reminds them, "was all that pasta and carrots and cat food bills and my Tabs."

"No we didn't," Pierre argues, holding the Marlboro between his thumb and index, the lit tip hidden in his cupped hand. "I never drank your Tabs then. They were full of saccharin and that isn't my style."

"*Wasn't* your style."

"Fine, it wasn't my style, then. But don't accuse me of robbing you six years ago."

Mary gets up to dump into the toilet the Marlboro butts that have been collecting in her ashtray since 5 P.M. She wishes Pierre would quit smoking—everybody knows that it's only a matter of days before he comes down with some kind of pulmonary cancer—but his style of smoking, his holding the cigarette as if it were a joint, makes her love him even more.

"Are joints still illegal in New York?" she asks Pierre and nostalgically hopes he will answer that yes, they are.

"No, I guess they are okay now," Pierre answers vaguely and then, to Tom, "aren't they?"

"Why care anyway, you guys haven't gotten stoned in five years. I swear, the next time you'll get to really start worrying 'bout it will be when your kids get stoned in your living rooms and you won't know what to do."

"I will know what to do," asserts Mary.

"Sock the little bastard in the jaw," jokes Tom, and Pierre seriously says to him, "Maybe, maybe you're right."

Tom's third wife has left him again and this time it's for good, she has announced. She sent him a postcard from New

Mexico and it said FOREVER MINE. Tom had loved her sense of humor: yet it sometimes backlashed.

Tom's first marriage was inconsequential, second year at Yale for him and freshman year for her. Once they were smoking and drinking in his room and she told him, "We should get married, I always wanted to get a husband in college." The same night they left New Haven on the New York–bound train and next morning, in a haze of hangover and smoky breath, they got married in front of a Spanish secretary and a retired judge. A surprised Yale housing officer, sure that theirs was one more undergraduate's clever scheme to obtain better dorm space, didn't believe them at first; only after Tom and Constance had repeatedly shown him their marriage license did the officer relent and give them a two-room apartment on campus. Thanks to all that space—rare in the usual scarcity of square footage that characterized student accommodations—Tom and Constance became known for having the wildest, largest parties. Beer kegs, not just beer cans, would be brought in; there would be giant-size plastic garbage pails holding electric Kool-Aid punch with dry ice smoking in it, four-foot-high bongs and hookas scattered throughout the two rooms, sometimes whole tanks of nitrous oxide stolen with the help of Pierre and Mary (Pierre and Tom acting as raiders, Mary as a lookout) from the biology or chemistry labs.

Strangers would find their way to Tom's parties, kiss Constance and hug Tom, use the marital bedroom and add their dope to the communal bowl on the floor. Tom loved it as long as it lasted: Constance loved it for only six months and eventually left him and moved in with a senior wide receiver. The receiver's parties did not last till dawn since he had to get up early for practice, and Constance spent her last three years at Yale badmouthing Tom and making sure he acquired a lousy reputation as a husband and human being among the Yale football team.

One day in his senior year Tom remembered that he and

Constance still had to get a divorce: their trip to New York City was the first time they had spent alone with each other in more than a year, and Tom thought that—if he tried really hard—he might even be able to get to love her. Constance's silence during the whole train ride and in the express subway that got them downtown let Tom know that trying would really not be worth it, after all.

Tom's second wife loved him and he loved her. But they were so full of love, it seemed, that everybody would be included and become involved in it, Tom and Flo passing their love around the way a child offers surplus candy to adults in a living room.

Looking at Flo, Tom would feel that everything had been given to him, too soon almost. Here he was, three years after college, no real job to speak of, and a wife who loved him more than anything else in the world: it scared him because he had never thought of himself as the marrying, husbandy kind. Their happiness and their love became as many ties for him, each "I love you so much" from Flo an additional dimension to the knots he felt were being tied around him: the knots that were holding him to the ground, choking him at the throat. And while Flo would continue to love him the same way she always had—more each day and spreading her love for him to the people around her—Tom began viewing other people as his way to freedom: his love for and with them not anymore a confirmation of his love for Flo but, rather, his own method for breaking loose from her.

He stopped telling her about what love had meant to him the previous night, he stopped saying "I love you" to her as they cooked, bathed, slept together, he stopped waiting in bed for her to wake up in the morning, he stopped showing his love for her. And Flo, like a plant that isn't watered anymore, began to dry up. They didn't fight or argue, no, they still believed in love—and might even still have loved each other too much to engage in real battles— but Flo also began to grow silent, and as silence grew, their love diminished imperceptibly, distilled drop by drop. All that was left at the end was just a bitter colorless residue, and—like dirt in a crystal—Tom and Flo's selective memories of the past hugeness of their love, of the vastness of it. Not of their love for each other, necessarily, just of their love, and of how they had lived it through each other.

Yet, once they separated and then got divorced, they felt drained, flushed out of love, and for months Tom would tell Pierre and Mary, "I don't feel anything now, I have become a simple perfect exemplar of alienation. Can you understand it? I can't even love you guys anymore." Pierre and Mary (both knowing Tom's strong recuperative capacities) would talk about it and reassure each other. Leaning against Mary's precariously balanced floor pillows, generic Italian wine in jelly glasses, they engaged in mutual comfort: "Give him a few weeks, he'll get over it." "Same ol' Tom, you'd think we're all still at Yale the way he acts." "It's not as if he was continuing to be in love with Flo or anything, after all."

But weeks and months had passed and Tom would still spend afternoons and evenings slouched on Pierre's couch, listless and babbling, telling them he still loved Flo, if only he had a second chance things would be different now, he had been too young—too blinded by his love and want of freedom—to really appreciate all that Flo had brought to him. He talked like an old man and Mary and Pierre started worrying about him. They set aside their own unhappiness and —therapeutically—devoted their energies to introducing Tom to as many unattached young women as they possibly could.

Tom didn't want to hear about it. Tom thought it was the stupidest idea the two of them had ever conceived—getting him stoned and wired with live estrogens. Tom refused to meet Carol and Sylvia and Jo-Ann until they, piqued and intrigued by a man who was determined to decline their company, called him up again and again and finally got to spend one wild night each in his apartment. Tom was not going to forget Flo just because he had grapefruit- and apple- and melon-shaped breasts paraded in front of him five or six nights a week. But gradually, it became clear, Tom grew to enjoy them, loved the guiltless pleasure that Mary and Pierre's address books were providing him. "Look, I ain't forgetting nobody," he would remind them. "It's not as if Flo didn't exist anymore; she's still one hundred percent in my brain, believe me." But then, as Mary pointed out, Tom's brain must have contained a lot more than one hundred percent.

Sarah had called Mary one February evening. "You know that guy you set me up with?" she asked, and Mary had felt the rush of annoyed déjà vu she had been experiencing more and more often since her female friends had been passing through Tom's hands: the confession about what an incredible lover he was, followed by the guarded "I don't know if I ought to thank you," the veiled question about whether Tom cared at all about human beings, the suggestion that maybe —after all was considered—he was just a sexist pig, and, finally, the real question: What did he really want, a toy, a lover, a girlfriend, a wife? "It's all up to you, I think," Mary would answer, determined to remain uncommitted and uninvolved until the end. Only sometimes, casting her restraints aside, she would add, "But I still wouldn't place marital hopes too high on the scale."

But Sarah sounded different: excited, anxious to thank Mary, she had invited Mary and Pierre to dinner, specifying that Tom would also join them. A surprise, almost a shock, to Mary.

Later that February—after she and Pierre had remarked that it had been a while since Tom had spent an afternoon joylessly getting stoned on their couch—they met in Sarah's kitchen and watched Tom help her chop basil and mozzarella for the sauce, saw him flash his old Tom grin at them, as if to say, "Hey, you guys, I've done it again!" And at twelve that evening, happy and replete with the veal pizzaiola, red wine, and knowledge that Tom could be himself once more, Mary and Pierre had genuinely come to believe that the bliss would last.

Even at Tom and Sarah's wedding, listening to the by-now stale "I do" from Tom, Mary and Pierre had held hands, beamed at Tom and Sarah's backs, and told each other, "This time he's got it, this time Tom's finally made it."

The four of them got into the habit of spending evenings together, cooking by rotation, lining up to buy cheap tickets for on- off- and off-off-Broadway shows, taking pride in preparing the strongest daiquiris and piña coladas while making sure (with a childish, jokingly perverted pleasure) that the others did not feel the staggering potency of the Bacardi until they got up from the table. They watched old movies on the VCR, each racing to utter the lines they could remember before they were said by the actors on the screen: not surprisingly, *The Wizard of Oz, Casablanca,* and *The Rocky Horror Picture Show* were their favorites when playing the game. It came as a surprise, however, that Mary also knew by heart the lines in *The Omen* and *The Exorcist:* surely an indication, Pierre argued, that Mary was not as psychologically together as she had always tried to appear.

"Fascination with the occult and being together have nothing to do with each other," Tom defended her.

"It has nothing to do with fascination or with being together," Mary added. "It's just that when a movie really strikes me I then remember it very well."

"And that's *exactly* what I was saying! You've got some weird, till now unknown, fascination with occult stuff. I have always known it," Pierre teased her. "Even at Yale you liked bizarre stuff," added Tom. "The only woman to ever read *all* of Gurdjieff... and the slower the Godard movie the better you liked it. You liked drilling rat brains in that 'Brains for Jocks' class of yours..." "You even liked cafeteria food," moaned Pierre. "And you *loved* the smell of bong water!" laughed Tom. "You practically used that shit as a mixer!" It was a mystery to all of them, including Tom, what kind of movies Sarah liked best.

"She *is* a total mystery, she's a question mark, the bi-i-i-g unknown," Pierre would complain to Mary. "Tom and

Sarah have been together for eight months already, and us together with them most of the time, and I still can't figure her out. What did you say, that she was a friend of yours before you went to Yale?"

"Sort of."

"Jesus, I can see why you'd 'sort-of' her. I mean, I like Sarah," Pierre explained, "she's got looks to kill, she seems to like Tom and Tom sure loves her so it should all be fine, right? But still that's not the feeling I get from the whole situation, from being with her that is."

"Don't make yourself paranoid about it, she's really totally okay, maybe just a bit shy," Mary would try to reassure him. She didn't really worry about Sarah but, rather, about Pierre: his constant slimness bordering on the malnourished, his nicotine-stained teeth and fingers, and, when he woke up in the morning, the brownish circles around his eyes and the dry deep cough, all further endeared him to her; all seemed to be a confirmation that she should indeed become Pierre's guardian angel.

"I want to know what she's all about," Pierre announced to Mary and Mary argued, "What do you want to do? Give her a Rorschach test, go for the open brain surgery?"

"Go for the late-at-night discovery," Pierre grinned and Mary felt dormant jealousy pangs awaken in her, stab her in the side of her head, in her guts. And though she had no claim over Pierre—friendship (and not their occasional love games) being the base of their relationship—she still fought out for herself, for Tom: "How could you do that to Tom? Now that he's finally in love again."

"Can't you think about *me,* for once? You're always concerned about Tom, I wonder if you even care about how *I* need to feel loved," Pierre barked back at her and Mary was stunned by Pierre's lack of understanding, by his genuine belief that she was doing it all for Tom, that it wasn't also Pierre and herself she was trying to protect.

"And anyway," Pierre continued, "I am not the pig you make me out to be. I'll talk about it with Tom first." When she was younger Mary had fought battles because she liked to fight, she had loved being the winner. Now, at twenty-eight, she often resolved not to engage in fights she knew she could not win. So Mary did not bother to argue with Pierre anymore.

She met with Sarah instead, a Mimosa brunch in SoHo. Sarah came into the restaurant more than fifteen minutes late, apologizing and looking perfectly made up. She walked as if she expected everybody to look at her and, yes, many men did. Determined to uncover the mystery and secret of Sarah's nature in the space of one Sunday brunch, Mary started constructing explanations right away. It was Sarah's looks: her maybe-antique Victorian clothes, the blue makeup that made her face seem even paler than it naturally was, her unfashionably long, almost white hair. It was Sarah's indiscriminate gaiety, the smiles that always seemed to be directed to a collective, her talk that—even when mordant—never seemed to offend anybody. It was Sarah's open and unusual acknowledgment that she was content with her life, that she loved it all—her looks, her mind, her friends, and the restaurants she had brunch in—though she still loved Tom more than anything else in the world. And maybe it was the sincerity with which Sarah seemed to let others know about her: if, that is, she did let them know.

That Sunday at 3:30 P.M., Mary left the brunch table and most of her uneaten eggs Benedict with the conviction that Pierre had in fact been right. She had spoken with Sarah for a full two hours but, still, she felt she knew almost nothing about her: so maybe Sarah truly was the kind of woman who could only be discovered late at night, after midnight, when two adults decide to bare their souls and show each other what they are really made of.

Tom and Pierre argued, they fought and spat unjust accusations at each other. Purposefully they lied because—though they would both have refused to acknowledge it—even while fighting each wanted to make sure that the other would remain his friend, each wanted to avoid uttering words in anger lest they prove themselves to be too real and reveal the other's faults and weaknesses.

Tom offered and promised Pierre everything he had, every woman he had known but Sarah. Pierre, as his purely investigative interest in Sarah waned, was beginning to feel a true desire for her grow in himself. Even after Tom and Pierre parted, each frustrated and unable to comprehend how his best friend could be so obtuse, so unsympathetic, Pierre dreamed about Sarah. It started as an unfocused fantasy, a rough outline of what Sarah would prove to be like naked and after midnight, and it rapidly evolved into a waterfall of graphic passion such as Pierre had not experienced since his early Yale days.

In the subway Pierre would see a long-haired woman cross her legs and he imagined Sarah sitting cross-legged at the edge of the bed waiting for him to join her. The slim woman who every Thursday bent across the counter to hand him the weekly cat food, the Puerto Rican teenager with peroxide blonde hair who lived downstairs, even the whores on Fourteenth Street with their blue makeup, they all, all, reminded him of Sarah, they were all there to tease him with their anonymous provocations. In class Pierre would look at his students (serious N.Y.U. freshmen who had chosen to study Russian mainly because of personal paranoiac beliefs about the future), and the face of a seventeen-year-old would become Sarah's, the student's smile Sarah's invitation to come close, the student's raised hand a poorly disguised attempt to attract Pierre's attention. And in its passion, his desire for Sarah evolved into an unbounded desire for all women he saw, for those he had not seen yet but could already imagine, for those he could not even imagine but who were almost ready to come knocking at his brain's doors. Sarah's image returned once again back to its original fluid state and Pierre discovered an indiscriminate—very carnal, and very real though up to then unknown to him—lust.

So Pierre turned into the Tom of long ago, the before-Sarah Tom, wanting more, content only when he was too exhausted to see anybody on Saturday night. But—unlike Tom—women would not follow Pierre home because of an unspoken promise that he would be the best lover they had ever experienced: they were attracted by Pierre's weakness, by that protective, almost maternal feeling that his lankiness and cough brought forward in them. Only later in the morning would Pierre's companions surprise themselves by thinking of him as a new lover and hope for another night with him. Each morning Pierre would lose his own identity as a wounded bird, but, by each evening, his own new identity had vanished once more and again he would find himself in bed with a woman who wanted to take care of him.

Only Mary had refused to second Pierre in his new passions. Rejecting Pierre's suggestions that she was just being jealous she thought of herself as genuinely concerned for his well-being. Sitting in Tom and Sarah's living room she spent hours arguing about the dangers of Pierre's new life-style, asking them to help her jolt him out of his new phase, all the while offering complicated and absurd psychological explanations to justify Pierre in her own eyes.

"You're right," Tom had once agreed, "the man is totally out of his mind. Figure that a couple of months ago he even came here to beg me to let him sleep with Sarah."

"He what?" asked Sarah, more interested, it seemed, than shocked.

"Didn't I tell you? Totally out of his mind, I swear. Came here with this wild look"—at which Mary laughed, "Maybe you're exaggerating"—"No, no, Mary, he was really wild and started telling me how he could not figure you out, Sarah, and how he had come to the conclusion that the only way to do it was to sleep with you. The way you discover if you're hanging 'round a vampire, I guess—wait till midnight and then check if his teeth have grown pointy." Tom snickered, reliving the absurdity of his conversation with Pierre.

"Poor Pierre," said Sarah very unexpectedly, and then to Tom, "You could at least have told me about it."

"What for?"

"Don't you think it was somewhat my business, that it kind of concerned me too, maybe?"

"Why, did you want to sleep with him? Is that what you're saying?"

"I'm not saying anything, " Sarah replied—rather loudly by now, and Mary whispered, "If you don't mind, I'm going," but nobody heard her—"I just don't understand why you had to keep it a secret. It's like reading somebody's mail and then regluing the envelopes to make sure they'll never know."

"This has got *nothing* to do with reading somebody's mail!"

"I really have to go," Mary whispered again.

"Then why didn't you tell me?" Sarah insisted.

"You know it now, isn't that enough? It's not too late, I can promise you. Better yet, Pierre is probably much hotter now that he's got so much more experience. I'm sure you'll both love it."

Mary was appalled: not only had she never heard Tom talk that way before, but she was beginning to question once again the future of Tom's marriage, beginning to worry about his happiness. And while she realized that—at that moment in time—neither she nor Pierre nor Tom felt content with their lives, while she almost felt sick with the sudden insight that their triadic closeness might forever prevent them from feeling real, total, lasting happiness, she heard Sarah say to Tom, "You're right, we just might love it." At that Mary had picked up her down jacket and left without even saying goodbye.

Pierre still showed up at Mary's apartment but there were too many silences between them. When Mary tried to remember what she and Pierre used to talk about, she could not come up with anything. There they were, clear in her mind, the images of her and Pierre sitting on the couch, around the kitchen table, in bed, moving their mouths as if talking. But no sound would come out of them, and she would be left in a fog, angry that her memory was failing her when she needed it most, when remembering was so important because—she was persuaded—only through recollection could she hope to resurrect and re-create what had once been between Pierre and herself.

"I want to show you something," Pierre had once told her, and making as if to kiss her he had blown into her mouth, his breath filling her lungs. She had been disgusted, upset that Pierre was using on her the stupid tricks he had learned during his inscrutable nights.

"But you would never have minded before!" protested Pierre, sincerely hurt by her reaction.

"Before is not now," Mary said, and then, as if to explain her use of a too obvious cliché, she added, "Things have changed, Pierre, haven't you noticed? Somehow it's not just you and I anymore—it's you and I and your two thousand other unknown women. Maybe that's good for you, we never promised anything to each other, but then spare me the repeats, okay?"

Still hurt, Pierre had seemed surprised, almost in shock at having only then realized that he had lost something important to him. Pierre—all of a sudden—looking to her more fragile than he had ever looked, and, while he started fumbling apologies, Mary had wanted so badly to hush him up, take him to her bedroom and love him the way she had loved him in the past. But she had not, she had not been able to find the words for it.

She had saved her words for Tom. Angry at both Pierre and Sarah and starved for Mary's nurturing, Tom sat on her couch, let her soothe him, caress his hair, and massage his back—just the way she had caressed and massaged Pierre before him. He let her hold him tight on the couch and then on the bed, and there they erased the pain of their mutual losses making hurt and unexpectedly furious love to each other, and then talking through the night.

In the morning they would not talk about each other, but about Sarah and Pierre. In the same and yet opposite way

133

in which—after Flo—Tom had tried to find comfort in numbers, he now attached himself to Mary. He found her caring, her anger, her concern for both Pierre and himself to be almost comforting. Strangely, he did not even mind that she continued to worry about Pierre: coming from Mary, it seemed to be the natural reaction, the correct one in the larger—almost cosmic—order of things in which all three were stuck.

At night they talked about themselves and explored each other with a domesticated fascination engendered by years of uncertain intimacy. "If I could tell you how much it all means . . . how all of this hurts, sometimes," Mary whispered.

"What hurts?"

"Never knowing where we stand, neither you nor me. Nor Pierre, for that matter." She sat naked in the bed facing him. "Maybe we are not letting ourselves be open and tell each other what we really mean and what we really want. Or maybe we are just not letting each other grow, but I don't know that I do want to grow, after all . . . I still don't know and you and Pierre are not making it any easier for me or for yourselves."

"I love you," said Tom to Mary and Mary chose not to hear him. It was easier, less painful that way.

In the morning Mary and Tom would become friends again and Tom would go back to his apartment and Sarah. He never asked her about Pierre. Neither Tom nor Mary really knew what—if anything—was happening between Pierre and Sarah. Tom grew philosophical, Pierre or anybody else, it did not really matter to him anymore. To his other friends he still seemed as happy and in love with Sarah as he had always been: they would be seen holding hands and kissing during VCR movies, smiling across the dinner table, biking with rehearsed and well-timed synchrony in Central Park. Only Mary was aware that Tom had already decided against his third—possibly his last—marriage. To her, he had confided his initial sudden hate for Pierre, the emptiness that again and again threatened to engulf him when he thought that it wasn't only Sarah's fault, that he really did not know Sarah, that he had maybe never known her, that he did not love her anymore. To Mary he had confided his surprise when Sarah told him that there had never been anything between Pierre and herself. And it was to Mary that he finally expressed his wish to see Pierre again.

"What about something like in the old times?" he simply asked. "Me and you *and* Pierre all together at dinner . . ."

They meet in a SoHo bar for before dinner drinks, and never get around to dinner. As in the old times they ask for improbable Manhattan cocktails—piña coladas, daiquiris, maitais—specifying they want them double, yes, very, very strong. They eat bowls of peanuts and green olives, and when Pierre kisses Mary—first on the cheek and then, tentatively, on the mouth—she accepts it as she had in the past; but this time she enjoys his kiss more.

"You have really become a better kisser—when you don't blow, that is," she teases him, and Pierre informs her, "Months of experience, my dear—they won't go to waste."

"Soon it'll be my turn," Mary says.

"We'll all be there for you," promises Tom and then kisses her, as if his turn—in front of Pierre—had finally come.

"Hey! What d'you think you're doing!" Pierre says. Tom shrugs his shoulders and answers, "Just let her have the best, will you?"

"You? Is that all the best she can have?" teases Pierre, but nobody laughs. In unison—as in a well-choreographed drama—they all grow dimmer, quieter.

"Maybe . . ." says Mary and Tom breaks the silence and calls, "Three daiquiris! Doubles!" to the waiter.

"Triples!" Pierre shouts, loud above the din of their SoHo reunion turf.

Happily drunk, waving and staggering under the fluid weight of the daiquiris, the three of them retire to Mary's apartment, the closest but also the more neutral choice.

There, forgetting their own identities and misery, they hug each other, a promise of eternal friendship renewed on Mary's purple couch.

"I don't think Sarah is going to hang around much longer," Tom tells them in a neutral voice.

"Sarah who?" asks Pierre, and they all—Tom included —laugh as if in relief.

"Do you guys want a joint?" Mary says, but then, even after a long search, she is unable to find any grass in her apartment. "Naah, it doesn't matter," Pierre reassures her, "I don't feel like smoking anyway."

"Good," Mary says, "because I really don't think I've got any grass around and, after all, the stuff I thought I had must be at least two years old."

"Ohmigod!" Tom feigns surprise, "Do you think . . . do you mean we're growing up?"

"No, I really don't think so," Mary tells Tom.

Alpine Sake

I was hiking through the Swiss Alps with my daughter, me in front and her following behind. I was careful not to let her understand that I was leading—she was eleven and did not accept being guided by me anymore. We walked around a large granite rock and then saw an old couple sitting on the ground. He must have been at least seventy-five, she perhaps five years younger than he. They were warming up something in a small metal pan, at first I thought it was soup and then I imagined it was some kind of tea—maybe an herb tea of Alpine weeds and flowers, another one of those wholesome and mostly bitter Swiss brews we had too often been made to drink during our stay.

They invited us to join them and motioned to me and Clara to sit down. The woman then apologized, warming up Sake in a metal pan was not the best method but it was the most convenient one at a two thousand meters height. Mentally I tried to figure out how many feet two thousand meters corresponded to and couldn't do it. I was unable to decide whether I had to divide or multiply. Strange, I thought: I am usually pretty good at figuring out foreign currencies and at calculating the best exchange rates, going from meters to feet or inches should not pose a problem to me. I felt surrounded by magic and Clara and I drank Sake from glass cups, the old couple from tin ones.

The old woman apologized again: they only had rice crackers to eat, would we care to have some? And though I was hungry I could not imagine taking our cheese sandwiches and chocolate out of the backpack and offering them around. They did belong and fit well in the Alps but somehow they seemed out of tune with what was happening to us. Even Clara, always hungry like most eleven-year-olds, did not ask for her sandwich and I was grateful to her for this unexpected display of tact.

Clara had never liked wine but she drank the Sake as if it were Coke, cup after cup, dipping into the old couple's seemingly bottomless supply. I should have minded, of course I should have, even then I knew that something was wrong. I am a responsible father: at home I make sure that Clara has finished all of her homework before she watches TV, that she does not eat more than her fair share of junk food. As a rule I do not let my little girl get drunk, especially under my eyes. But I felt only surprise and wonder and maybe a little embarrassment. No guilt, no responsibility anymore, here on the alp with my child and the Sake.

They never seemed to pour any more Sake from the bottle into the pan: yet we drank and drank (Clara, and I, and the two old people) and there was always plenty. "Enough!" I wanted to shout at a certain moment (saying it in a normal voice would not have been sufficient to break the enchantment that had been woven around us). "Enough! We came here to hike, to walk, not so that I could get drunk with my daughter. Please let us go, Clara, let's leave." Yet I was unable to utter those words: Clara and I remained there, sitting on the rocky ground drinking Sake.

In the summer the Alps are of two non-primary colors: green where grass and trees grow (dark shadow green at times, at times light sun-bright green punctuated by wild flowers); and brown-grey above the tree line, with rocks and earth sharing the scorched bounty of the sun. But, as I looked around, there was little green to be seen. There were trees and grass and rocks, but all had been brushed in yellow, a yellow that did not blend with the blue of the sky to form green. Everything looked dry and lifeless, everywhere casualties of the mountain's rarefied oxygen. Yellow surrounded me and made it almost impossible to focus. I cannot be drunk, I thought, nothing is spinning around me yet: the earth is as still as it can be and I and Clara are at the center of it.

"You have beautiful child," the old man told me, and without knowing why, I felt more threatened than flattered by his statement. Ordinarily I would have accepted it as a normal, indeed deserved, compliment. Clara *is* very pretty and I like people to notice and acknowledge her beauty although I am rather ambivalent about their doing it in front of her.

But, the Sake cup tight in my hand, I read evil intentions in the man's assertion. He wanted what I wanted—what was mine, only mine, mine to give and mine not to give. Waves of saturated yellow swayed across my eyes. I'm drunk, I thought, disgustingly and dangerously drunk. Should stop drinking Sake, it's really stronger than I remember it to be . . . should at least try to eat something . . .

"Yes, she's really a pretty child," the old woman confirmed. I looked at Clara, recognizing the gnawing feeling of danger that had developed in me, but nevertheless said, "She is, she's something special."

Clara returned my gaze, her clear aqua eyes resting on me for a long, comfortable time, steady on my face and body. Momentarily, I was afraid that my own skin could melt under the intensity of my child's look. But then I saw a whisper of smile flow across her lips, a twinkle of amusement breeze in her eyes: the signals with which daily she acknowledges her understanding and confirms our complicity. Not only was she absolutely aware of my uncomfortable delight, but she was pleased by it and enjoyed the situation as much as I. She would, I could tell, be ready to do anything to make the moment last forever.

I love my child, I told myself, and today she is almost a miracle. She is special, but you shouldn't let them know it: make them believe she's ordinary, protect her, do it for your own sake as well as Clara's. For your own sake, I thought, and I was overtaken by mirth, for my sake and for their Sake, the paradoxical sameness of the words now offering up till then undiscovered ridiculous possibilities. "But," I told myself, "for the sake of their Sake and thus for your very own sake you may lie about Clara, even though it means betraying her. Lie—she is waiting for you to do it, for you to make her special and draw her in makeup colors. For all the sakes and Sakes on this alp and for those that will follow let them believe she is so much more than just the pretty child they think she is, more than the evident Clara, than the pretty child she *really* is."

Lie. Because what I should have told them, what I still sincerely wanted to say was, "Clara is really not what she appears to be, she's a common almost-adolescent, the kind you'll find chewing pencils and erasers in every sixth-grade in every American public school, the kind who'll always order gooey ice cream sundaes and burgers with extra ketchup and no pickle at every car stop on every highway, she is as ordinary and as much as an 'every' child as you'll ever be likely to encounter. . ." But I was afraid that, had I opened their eyes to this fact, the Sake would have stopped flowing. I was ready—though at the time I did not know how to put it into words—to prostitute an eleven-year-old child for a bottomless cup of Sake.

I would never have believed myself capable of such an action, nor, had anybody ever suggested I could, would I have peacefully accepted the insult. But, like a New Orleans madame getting the youngest child ready for her first dollars, like the drunkard father of every Kerouac and Cassady book, I wanted more than anything to remain there on the anonymous Alps with our anonymous hosts and drink their Sake.

Clara continued to sit still on the rock she had first sat on, moving only her arm to bring the cup up to her lips. I turned my head away from her and nodded slightly at the old couple, smiling almost sheepishly not at anybody in particular but because I needed to believe that I could still smile, that I was a nice guy who would not betray anybody (not a generous couple of mountain climbers, not my daughter), and especially not for a drink.

I don't usually drink. My wife does: she drinks Bloody Marys at lunch, needs her cocktails of dry martinis and red Camparis, white wine at dinner with the fish, red with the meat, cognac and Calvados after the meal. She sips small sips and stares at us—at me and at Clara—as if we were her enemy. I don't drink but take care of Clara. I let Clara rest her head on my shoulder and on my chest when it's late at night and we can't fall asleep. I carried her to bed when she was a child: now I can't do it anymore. At home Clara walks up to her bed alone and I watch her walk upstairs as I sit still on the living room couch.

My love for Clara (my only child, the little girl I had wanted with all my heart, that I knew would be given to me even before she was ever conceived) is boundless, and yet somehow manages to grow with every passing day. While my wife's image (tarnished by glasses of spirits and wine, diluted by her silence and passive jealousy) grows increasingly dimmer, Clara's shines brighter. I have been told by concerned friends that I am not being fair to my wife, that my choice was to be wedded to her and not to be married to my daughter. But it is a matter of pure moral and esthetic justice: the most beautiful, the wisest, the purest always wins, and Clara has no match in this contest nor will she ever have.

I love Clara and I would rather die than see her hurt, or

141

know that I could ever be an instrument of her pain. I noticed that at the bottom of my cup remained only a few drops of Sake and, almost with horror, I heard myself repeat, "Oh yes, she's special, she's lovely, more than you can imagine; she really *is* beautiful." And then, looking at Clara's knowing eyes, I realized that she understood perfectly why I was so shamelessly and bluntly singing her praises. And that, having surreptitiously been transformed into a little alcoholic slut, she consented to my maneuvers; she was actually proud to be the instrument of my strategy.

But by then the woman had stopped asking us if we cared for some more Sake every time a refill was needed; she correctly surmised that refills were not only welcome but almost necessary, that Sake had become our reason for remaining on that mountain, for foregoing our planned hike and eventual picnic.

And she was smiling at the old man—her husband, I assumed, although nothing yet had been said—a conspiratorial smile that proved that she herself was also aware of my intentions, and that they should get ready for the next step. I had almost come to think of myself as cunning, a master at obtaining all the Sake I wanted without any direct communication, but in fact I had become more transparent, and thus more vulnerable, than I had ever been in my adult life. I braced myself for what would follow, ready for any coming surprise, and yet unwilling to let go of my Sake cup. Clara's blue eyes the only contrast in the sea of yellow, my anchor as—minute by minute, hour by hour—I was becoming more and more gloriously intoxicated by the brilliance of each and every one of the Sake's almost supernatural qualities.

Because it was not—or not only, should I say?—the drunken feeling that the Sake provoked in me that had rendered it so necessary. Nor was it only its exotic essence—the magic of its endless flow, the wild setting in which we were drinking it, which led me to want and silently demand more, more please! again, again! more!—but its very taste, the nature of the Sake itself. It was like none I had ever drunk before, smooth to the point of creaminess, faintly spicy as if the wild Alpine herbs had been incorporated in its flavor, warm enough to be almost scalding and yet never once burning my lips. Drinking it was pure, undiluted pleasure of the kind one never expects to find and experience, or maybe can only see advertised in cheap populistic renditions of Catholic heaven. Or, I thought, in the sophisticated hell of hallucinated millenarian monks; as such I was ready to do anything to obtain access to that hell, to make it last and last and last . . .

More and more Sake, more Sake for me and my darling, my Clara, whose transformation I was becoming increasingly aware of. Her cheeks were flushed, her brow and forehead glistening with odorless prepubescent perspiration (have I forgotten to mention that it was a particularly hot day?), her eyes becoming moister, shining brighter; all in all a delightful combination, the unexpected result of the novelty and concentration of the alcohol in her young body.

She sat as still as ever, both hands cupped around the glass as if to steady it and control it, silently sipping Sake and watching us—not just me by now but all of us, the adults. Silently sipping, I say, but we were all silent. None of that usual Alp talk about erratic weather, colorful mountain flowers, best hot chocolate and best fondue spots in town. Rather, every so occasionally, our silence would be broken with one of us stating in a matter of fact way that my daughter was a delight, that I must consider myself lucky . . . one of us offering more rice crackers with one single word: "Care . . . ?" One of us emitting a whispered sigh of pleasure, the only concession to expressing the bliss we felt . . .

When will it ever stop? I wondered, and, once again, I wanted to shout, "Never!" and, simultaneously and incongruously, shout, "Now! Now, please make it stop now!" Please let it never stop, I prayed, let me remain here where there is no measure of time, where deep, thick, joy lasts and lasts and lasts . . .

I shifted myself on my rock, moving closer to Clara's. She removed one hand from the glass cup and placed her arm on my shoulders. I lingered under the weight of her arm and, all the while, some of the earth's saturated yellow began to give way to a paler, warmer shade. Yet I could see little of it. I was unable to focus on anything except single details . . . the feeling of Clara's arm, my hand caressing her child-thin hair, the yellow-brown rock she was sitting on, the perfectly spherical shape of our Sake cups. "Daddy," I think I heard Clara say. Her voice was a bit weary, a bit hoarse. She sounded so young and almost lost. "Petite . . ." I said to her, using the nickname she adores, "Ma petite, what do you want, what can I give you?" This is what I wanted her to do: I wanted her to ask for more Sake please, to hand me her cup to fill.

My cup was still full, the Sake still warm. Clara motionless and, never more than now, mine. The woman spoke. She said, "I think it's time for us to get up, walk for a while." Shocked and in a stupor, I looked away and I saw colors. I noticed that the sky had turned opaque, dark purple-blue; that the air was cooler, almost cold. There was nothing we could do: we were being betrayed by the night, tricked when all I wanted then was to remain near the Sake, warm my mouth and my blood with its liquid heat, warm my hands around the glass, untangle my child's smooth hair with my fingertips.

We had no voice in the matter. The old man murmured something unintelligible to the old woman and, without consulting me or beautiful Clara, slowly and methodically began to assemble the objects around us. In the orderliness of his actions I detected an almost sacred aura, similar to that surrounding the Japanese tea ceremonies: it was fitting, I thought, that such an aura be created for yet another Japanese drink. My mind generated for my amusement a ridiculous image — that of Italian peasants celebrating a tea ceremony around a fiasco of Chianti; I vividly saw the scene in its every detail, the large peasants with dirty muddy clothes bowing in front of a bottle containing that glowing, red, heavy liquid. I burst out laughing and tried to explain the cause of my merriment to my companions. But none seemed to hear me, or to be able or willing to understand me.

They gathered everything: the gas heater that—surprisingly—was only slightly warm to the touch; the pan that suddenly contained not a trace of Sake anymore; the tin cups and the glass cups, which they removed from our hands; the plastic bags that had held the rice crackers—translucent and covered with Japanese writing. I should have picked up my backpack but was reluctant to do so, consciously willing that, if I only stalled long enough, the exodus would not take place. Clara seemed to be in a similar state of mind, determined to prevent the imminent departure.

"We *should* hurry up," the old man prodded, in an almost pleading tone, "It'll be dark soon." And though that might well have been the perfect moment to break free of the spell, like a spoiled child I replied, "Nights are beautiful on the Alps, there's no reason to leave so soon." All the while looking at Clara with new eyes (not bothering to exercise the usual paternal check to make sure she was not cold in her T-shirt and shorts, but just observing her beauty and youth —the initial shivering of her body and the emerging goose pimples on her arms becoming further details in my admiration), thinking that in front of me, there sat quite a beautiful child. Beautiful child, I say, not lovely daughter: there is a real difference between the two and, even then, I was keenly aware of it. Even then, I am sure, she was aware of it too.

She was my daughter, the person for whom this evening's miracle had been performed, the woman at my side, the child who had always confided in me and in whom I had always confided. She looked at me with eyes that recognized that the Sake had taken possession of us, that warned me that we should not let go of it.

But there they stood, the old man and the old woman, towering above us. Clara and I had remained seated on our respective rocks though I am sure that had one of us risen the other would have followed. "Come," the man patiently prodded us, "it's time. Rise, come." The time, I thought, the time has come. It has come and it's here, and in my mind the phrase echoed and was repeated again and again, tumbling from one corner to the other of my head until all of it was full of its sound, the time has come the time has come the time has come it's here it's here, my whole body numbed by its rhythmic obsession.

The time has come and you don't know where you are and you don't know what time it is and what time is and what is becoming of you and of your daughter. Your daughter, remember? Clara with the aqua eyes who sees and knows so much more than she should. The time has come for you and Clara, the time is here, come. You and Clara, come.

The spell had once more been woven around me, and again I struggled to free myself of its obscene lure, vainly struggled, that is, because I very well knew that I had no desire to escape it. And all the while panic in me grew more intense than ever, treacherously hitting me in my stomach and in my groin, perfidiously insinuating itself in my throat until I could not breathe anymore, until I had to bend my body and almost split it in two because the pain of fear and the pain of desire and the pain of cowardliness and that of sin and desire again were too much for one body alone to bear, until I wanted with all my soul and all my being to be sick —as sick as I had ever been—and get rid of the Sake, of the old man and woman, and remain alone with my Clara and with her alone descend from our mountain.

They stood in front of us, offering their promises, and looking at Clara. She let both arms hang on her sides, placed her hands steadily on the rock, palms down to support the oblique weight of her raising body: she was ready to go. I followed her example, got up in a wobbly uncertain motion, and came to stand near her. Tentatively, timid now that the spell had been broken, I let my hand rest on the nape of her neck. Almost imperceptibly, she flinched—a shy, rapid movement that Clara herself seemed to fail to notice. Her nape was damp, and I marveled at the fact—the evening chill should have been sufficient to let her perspiration dry off by now. Only later did I realize that Clara's sweat was not a prolonged or late reaction to the day's heat, but a true, almost animal, reaction to fear.

Like a sacred procession descending a mountain to carry the Saint back to the village, we walked toward the lights in the valley below us. In silence, in almost total darkness, we shuffled our feet on the Alpine rocks, we dragged our puzzled bodies downhill. Clara and I walking at the back of the little line, attempting to identify our position and direction within a territory we both knew well, but which the night had rendered alien and transformed into a mystery. I was aware that I did not know where we were going, that the old couple had become our guides for the day and for the night. Again, how easy it would have been to break free, our hotel was in the village, home was but a few minutes away . . . and yet their pull was too strong, their lead inescapable. I had let myself become possessed and had forgotten my responsibility to my child. For a while she had been mine but only half a child . . . the other half? I don't know, I did not want to know.

"Clara," I called, but the child who walked in front of me did not turn and did not stop. "Petite," I said, but my voice was slurred and spittle dribbled out of my mouth as I struggled with the "t"s of the word. I tried to call her again but by now any production of sound demanded a will and an effort that I did not have in me anymore. My head thumping, my brain was so clogged that no light could penetrate it, no sight was accessible to me. I kept walking mechanically, a blind and stupid android vainly trying to call out to Clara and warn her of the Sake, of the old couple, and of myself. I think my knees gave way when I noticed that we had stopped walking and that I was standing in front of some kind of building with the stocky shape and heavy, slanted proportions of a Swiss chalet.

I found myself at the center of a living room, but had no memory nor understanding of how I had ever gotten there. The room was scarcely furnished. The only objects within it were a series of rigid wooden chairs, bare of any pillows or other item that could have suggested a preoccupation with esthetics or a concession to comfort. No paintings on the walls, no table near the chairs, no cigarette butts or empty glasses to denote that somebody (anybody) had ever lived in that room. Just an almost obsessive fastidious cleanliness throughout. I did not know what led me to call it a living room, no room this bare should ever be called "living"; yet I began to dimly recall that as I had entered into it somebody had whispered to me that that was the living room. I had believed him (her? it? the voice I mean . . .), but why shouldn't I have? I was ready to believe anything by now. That I had been drugged and hypnotized, that I had been led to see and think and maybe even act (please god no, not act . . .) what is more than forbidden, what is unspeakable and inhuman. I tried to bring Clara back into my consciousness but her image escaped me.

I had been standing for I don't know how long a time and, following what had for me been an arduous walk down the mountain, I wanted to lie down, curl my body into protection and sleep. The nausea of fear mixing with the nausea of sleep, and though I struggled to remain awake, though I did not want to forget Clara, my will had already lost too many battles that day and could not hope to triumph in any. My knees gave way and I simultaneously fell to the floor and fell asleep.

I dreamed, sleeping the solid and massive sleep that follows extreme alcohol consumption. Periodically, Clara's face would intrude in my mind and, with uncanny vividness, I would recognize every detail and then know that it could be no reproduction or mask of my baby but only her, only Clara. Why she flashed into my sleep I do not know, hers was a filial haunting that I was unable to refuse or escape. But because of her intrusion, my sleep did not provide me with the liberating respite I needed. Time and time again, through the waves of throbbing nausea that flushed throughout my body, I struggled to protect my sleep from Clara's presence. In the end, I simply did not make it.

As I awoke I found myself at the exact center of the barren room, and my first sensation was the uncomfortable soreness of my whole body: the spine—twisted throughout the whole night in a fetal position—was unable to model itself into a vertical and erect state, my knee joints creaked like rusty metal when I tried to extend my legs, even my shoulders could not readapt themselves to bear the natural weight of my dangling arms. And my parched throat and pasty mouth were furiously demanding water, my empty stomach crying out for food, my mind pleading for more and better sleep. Overall a most unpleasant set of sensations, such that the state of my body prevented me from concentrating on what were more urgent and pressing problems.

Clara. Sake. Where was I? And what about the old couple, who were they? What was I supposed to do now, wait or try to escape? But I did not know where I was nor why . . . And what had happened yesterday, what had happened of yesterday's Sake, was there more, *was there* (anywhere, anyplace) more to be gotten and drunk? Or, I raged in a degenerate impetus of selfishness, was Clara enjoying the Sake, *my* Sake, while I stood here wishing for more and worrying about her? I should worry more about her, I thought, she is a child, she is so young; I have to be more of a father to her. She needs my protection and not only my love—but, somehow, I did not want to think about it and my head ached so . . .

I finally chose the only logical course of action and— after peering from the window and noticing that the world was once again in order, that green meadows speckled with chocolate-colored cows led to conventional grey-brown mountains—I checked the door. To my surprise it opened with ease: I was not a prisoner. Still hesitant, I stepped out, walked down a flight of stairs, and remained still, facing a long and white hallway punctuated by a row of identical white wooden doors. Behind one of these doors stood Clara, behind another the Sake; maybe they were already together, enjoying each other's company, my child ritually pouring the hot Sake into her little glass cup. In my mind, the bloody and gruesome memory of the Bluebeard tale of my childhood: one door that cannot be entered, one door that leads nowhere, one door hiding the blood-soaked remains of female victims, one door—only one—that offers salvation but you can never tell which door is which and which key will open the right one.

First door: an empty white room, swept clean and bare, an open window letting in the cool mountain air. I paused in the room for a few too-short minutes breathing deeply, hoping that if I charged my lungs with enough oxygen my whole body and mind would wake up.

Second door: the hinges squeaked with an unnatural loud noise and I became convinced that, now that everybody had been made aware of my presence, I would be caught then and there, tried and executed on the spot. Second door, the consciousness of the complete unknown into which I had been plunged, the renewed beginning of my fear. Again, the room was bare—nothing but a stripped foam mattress on the floor. No sheets or pillow, a closed window. I did not linger: I did not want to be found and forced to stop my search.

Third door: locked. I was afraid, uncertain, as to what action I should take. I looked around for the presence of a possible stray key, the first of the Bluebeard keys. And though it was on the floor right next to my feet, I congratulated myself: I had found the key, I would soon also find my child. Third door, third room: two leather suitcases on the floor, lying open side by side. They were empty but, by now, their empty presence seemed to be absolutely reasonable.

Fourth door: the surprise of a fully furnished room, deceptive, almost a lie in the schema of things I had experienced until then. A bed (more of a cot, really) covered by a worn, bleached bedspread; a wooden closet with its doors half open, revealing piles of carefully folded horse blankets; a table and a wooden chair identical to the ones that my living room had contained; two faded color prints on the walls, each depicting a different cow lying in a lush green field. And a full-length mirror placed against the wall, invincible temptation for me to remain in the room and look at my mirror image. I expected to see myself transformed, uglier and older, but it was not so. I was almost disappointed. Aside from looking more tired than usual I was the same as yesterday: my looks could easily have been the boring result of a weekend of drunken amusement. Unwilling to face the possibilities of the ordinary I left the room.

Fifth door: one more barren room. Ready to close the door I caught sight of four small cups—two glass cups and two tin cups—stranded on the wooden floor. I entered into the room and took a glass cup into my hand. And though I held it and examined it at length, though I believed with all my senses and with all the strength of my intuition that the cups were the same ones from which we had drunk Sake the day before, my memory could not verify the fact. Handling the cup delicately, fingering its contours and the roughness of the glass, I was like a lost explorer observing his broken compass, superstitiously trusting that it would regain its magnetic integrity and provide me with the proof I needed. Yet I failed in the task. The cups had to remain without a definite history, and the fifth room offered to me only crumbs of confirmation of what might have been, but no truth in which to believe.

Sixth, seventh door: the same emptiness everywhere (a towel fell with a muffled thump when I turned the handle of the seventh door, an unexpected and almost menacing sound, the first to break the complete silence in which I moved). Eighth door and, hidden in a corner, my backpack. I think I screamed, a scream of joy and thanks for recognition of the familiar. I rushed to the backpack, opened its front flap and burrowed into its contents, listening to the crackling sound of the crumpled wax paper in which I had wrapped the sandwiches, feeling the cool smoothness of the aluminum foil around the chocolate bar. I had found reality and I had found food . . . I tore the foil surrounding the chocolate and let my hunger take over. I forgot Clara, the Sake, the queer emptiness of my surroundings.

I ate all the chocolate, biting furiously into it, not bothering to chew. It was energy and strength for the journey I was sure still lay ahead. But I was more lucid, more determined now. I would not repeat yesterday's irresponsible mistakes; I would not let myself get drunk in front of my child nor let her do the same in front of me. I would find her, comfort her, lead her out of this house and—no matter how tempting—neither of us would stop for any more Sake. My thirst became immense, overwhelming. Holding on to the backpack, I left the room to look for some water, a bathroom maybe. I needed a drink.

I had to open several more doors to find one with a faucet. In their whiteness and bareness all the rooms were identical, almost indistinguishable. I had become bolder by now and I had lost my reluctance to make any noise. I opened doors with a kick, closed them with a bang. I swore aloud as the sound of my hiking boots echoed in the hallway. In a white-tiled bathroom I drank heavily from the faucet and peed with prolonged force. I walked out drying my hands on my jeans, and Clara was waiting at the door, sleep in her eyes and a toothbrush in her hand.

I did not know what to do: the familiarity of the scene (her waiting for me to come out of the bathroom in the morning, sleepily and impatiently awaiting her turn) was such that it did not allow me to experience the full extent of my surprise. What astounded me was the immaturity of her looks, the child reflected in the puffiness of her eyes and in her tousled uncombed hair. Yesterday she had seemed ripe for any fantasy, the perfect teasing example of a child's subtle power. Today she stood in front of me and I could see that her legs sticking out of her shorts were still way too short, her chest boyishly flat, her head proportionately too large for her body; I could see that she herself still had so much growing up to do, and *this* surprised me more than her very presence had.

"Clara," I murmured slowly. I was very tired, I wanted to sleep where I could be sure Clara would be, where I would never risk losing her again. With fatherly concern I embraced her sleepy body, holding and hugging her tight until she tried to squirm away from me in her typical embarrassed eleven-year-old way. Then she rested her face on my chest and I detected the lingering odor of Sake on her breath, the musty smell of the mountain earth on her hair.

I wanted her to stay with me, I needed to ask her so much, but she slipped into the bathroom without a word. From my side of the door I listened to the comforting everyday noises, the tap water running, the flush of the toilet, her brushing and gargling. We weren't home but we were together. Waiting, I rehearsed the questions I would ask her: who had given her the toothbrush? where had she slept? how did she feel, and had anything happened to her during the night? I had one of yesterday's sandwiches for her if she was hungry, there was nothing to be afraid of now . . . all questions culminating with the most pressing and delicate of them all, was she thirsty, did she know if *(where)* more Sake could be gotten?

How could I be so insensitive? Easy, the sight of Clara— healthy, unspoiled, childish Clara—had reassured me as to the lack of danger in the absurd reality of the situation I was living: I did not have to worry about her anymore, she was near me (just where I wanted her to be), she looked the way I wanted her to look. I could worry about myself now, and that worry had taken the form of more Sake; Clara's breath had only served to accentuate my need.

She came out of the bathroom wiping her face with the front end of her T-shirt. She was by now fully awake: she looked at me solemnly and then, still without a word, she moved away, walking the whole length of the hallway to disappear down a flight of stairs. I ran after Clara, retracing my steps as I passed in front of an almost infinite number of closed white doors then down a stairway that I had failed to notice before, only to find myself in a hallway identical to the one I had just left. It's a joke, a flashback, I thought, it is one more hallucinatory gift from the Sake. I see what I have already seen and Clara has disappeared again.

I called out for Clara using the whole loudness of my voice, fearful that I might not be given a second chance to find her. I was standing at the end of the hallway bellowing, yelling for my child to come. My voice had never been so loud, and the sound of her name reverberated throughout the whole house and in my own skull. I wanted my baby with water on her face, my child with the toothbrush, the little girl who saw through me and still loved me, Clara with the sweet Sake breath . . .

And as I cried out her name again and again a door opened, sunlight invaded my hallway and, in the frame of the door, I saw Clara's dark silhouette. I was momentarily blinded by the pure intensity of the light on the Alps but, as I stepped outside, I saw the coarse green-yellow mountain grass, an impossibly clear blue sky, Clara, and the old couple.

"Clara!" I called out to her and for the second time that day I held her tight against my chest, vowing I would never let her go. "Baby, why did you run away?" I was obviously embarrassing her, yet I sincerely did not give a damn about hurting her eleven-year-old sensibility: all I wanted was to take her away, all I wanted was her and more Sake. And an explanation, maybe.

I faced the old couple with undisguised hostility. "Would you like some breakfast?" the man asked me in a cordial tone. Though he might have failed to detect my mood it was likely that he had decided to overlook it. "I'd like some explanations," I curtly replied. He gave an audible sigh and remained silent. "I would like to know," I insisted, all the while holding Clara's arm, afraid that she would escape me as she had done before, "why we are here."

"You were, you will excuse me for saying so, simply too—let me be blunt—drunk for us to allow you to walk to your home alone," the woman informed me. I was not surprised by her answer, it reflected what I had expected one of them to say. Indeed, I had wanted them to say it, so as to be able to ask the next logical question.

"Drunk on what?"

They both giggled and Clara moaned, "Daaad," so I

sharply ordered her to shut up, the stakes were too important to allow a child to spoil the game. The man said in a most natural tone of voice, "Sake, of course," adding teasingly, "have you already forgotten what we told you yesterday on the mountain?"

"It wasn't Sake," I replied, "you know that as well as I do."

"So," the woman wanted to know, "if it wasn't Sake what was it then?"

"*You* tell me what it was!"

"It was Sake, I just told you so . . ."

"And do you expect me to believe you?"

The old man seemed tired, sat on the yellow-green ground and answered, "You can believe what you want, it's all up to you, it's all in your hands."

"In your head," added the woman.

"What game are you playing?" I shouted and held on even more strongly to Clara's thin wrist, feeling her frightened pull as she struggled to break free from me.

"What do *you* want?" the man asked me, looking at me with his tired gaze.

And so, mesmerized by his performance, I mumbled the most inane, innocent, and incongruous thought: "Where did Clara get that toothbrush?" and as I asked I felt ashamed of my own stupidity.

"You really want to know?" the woman answered, offering me the gift of a second chance.

"No. Not really. So then tell me, where did the so-called Sake come from?"

The woman shook her head, as if unable to believe that I could still be so obtuse. "From there," she said, her whole hand pointing to the house behind me, "there are dozens of bottles of Sake in the hotel cellars." I turned around and over my head I read the engraved writing PENSION ALPINA and, right underneath it, on a cardboard sign dangling from the front door handle SOMMER GESCHLOSSEN..

"Would you like to take home a couple of bottles?" the

155

man asked me, immediately adding, as if trying not to offend, "a gift from me and my wife, of course . . ."

I looked at Clara now standing still and calm near me and the old wave of fear made itself known in my stomach, just the faintest blip of nausea and uncontrollable passion. Two simultaneous and yet contradictory fears, one that of reliving the magic within my very own four walls — just me and Clara and who knows if I would have safely continued to view her as my baby child? — and the other, opposite fear of being unable to find the bliss anymore, of coming to realize that it had been nothing but rice water dirtied by seventeen percent methyl.

So I said, no, no thank you, we really have to get home, they are waiting for us down at the village, and without bothering to answer Clara's interrogative protests ("Who? Who, Daddy? *Nobody's* waiting for us, who's waiting, Dad?") I started walking away from the hotel, heading downhill toward the distant houses I recognized.

After a couple of minutes I turned around, almost believing that I would see there was no Pension at all, that I would discover that the chalet itself had been a mental trick, an hallucinatory farce. But everything was still there, the cows and the chalet and the old couple staring not at us but at each other. So I looked at Clara walking by my side, kneeled to remove the backpack from my shoulders, and handed her a stale cheese sandwich. I thought I still miss the Sake, I already miss it. But, I thought, but I have my baby, I have Clara with me, after all. I thought yes, I don't have the bliss of the Sake but I have Clara and my love for her. Yes, I thought, I have enough, love is a dangerous drug.

The Light
in the Window

She walked out of the weekend house and found two dead blackbirds on the front porch: they must have banged into the bedroom window during the night, and she hoped that the concussion had been strong enough to kill them on the spot. Poor birdies, she thought, all the while disgusted by the blood that trickled out of one blackbird's open yellow beak. She stood still, waiting for Jonathan to join her, knowing that he would take care of them. She stared at their feathers fluttering in the fringe of cold wind the night's storm had left behind, and wondered if they really were blackbirds after all: for all she knew they could have been ravens or magpies. She was a city woman, she reminded herself.

Jonathan came out the front door in his T-shirt and jogging shorts. He never jogged—actually despised people who took too much care of their own bodies—and viewed this attitude as reflecting perfectly his own intellectualism. She did not care about his ridiculous misconceptions; Jonathan's body could stand very well on its own without any help from jogging. Sometimes she thought that in fifteen years Jonathan would surely have a paunch and sagging shoulders: it didn't bother her, the chances that she and Jonathan would still see each other in fifteen years were so slim as to be practically nil. The chances, she thought, that she and Jonathan would still see each other in two months' time were just as slim.

Jonathan didn't see the dead birds, he was looking only at her through his grey eyes. This early in the morning his eyes were smaller than usual and he was squinting in an attempt to squeeze the leftover sleep out of them. When she told him, "Look!" he did not look down at the ground but up to the sky, as if seeking meteorological confirmation that today was going to be another wet day and they would spend it cooped inside the house—just she and he alone on the Jersey shore. She repeated, "Look!" and her hand pointed to the birds at her feet. Jonathan followed the hand's direction and she saw him recoil momentarily when he spotted the birds.

"We should give them a decent burial," she said to Jonathan, all the while feeling irksomely immature, in her head the remembered sadness and pleasures of childhood's pet burials. Jonathan looked at her as if she were out of her mind. "It's the trash can, darling," he said. "If you want to dig 'em a grave you'll have to dig it on your own." What a mean insensitive bastard Jonathan was, she thought. Just the kind of man she always ended up being stuck with: selfish, uninterested in her needs, spending time with her because she was good company and not because of who she was. "Goodbye," she said to him and started walking toward the beach, hoping all the while that he would have the good sense not to follow her.

She should have known better; Jonathan always followed her although he would never have admitted to the fact. Nor did he see it as "following"—the word did not mean anything to Jonathan: he simply wanted to be with her, be wherever she was. Once, in one of her frequent moments of rage, she had turned to him and yelled, "Stop following me!" and had then seen the look of genuine disbelief on his face. Jonathan, she had thought, has no conception that he is following me: he is like a gosling, irrevocably imprinted on its mother and totally unconscious of it. For a while the tenderness evoked by this thought had appeased her, she had looked at Jonathan as her own baby bird, she had grown less impatient toward him. But by the end of the month she had been ready to shake him off once again: baby geese and baby birds eventually grew up but Jonathan never did. He would always be there, always wanting her presence and her company, always ready to run after her. It had struck her as unfair and she abandoned the comforting image of Jonathan as a helplessly attached animal.

So, as she walked to the beach, she became aware that Jonathan was coming behind her, walking fast. With increasing clarity she could hear the sound that announced him approaching: Jonathan was not wearing any shoes—as was his fashion on the shore from April to October—and the suction of his bare feet against the wet pavement generated a muffled popping noise at each step. She turned around to face him and yelled, "What are you doing here! I want to be alone! And I don't want to see those birds when I come back!" As the words left her mouth she realized that they had not conveyed her anger: rather, hers had been a childish wail, of the petulant "I wanna buy candy. . ." variety. She tried to repair the mistake by offering an explanation to Jonathan: "They upset me, those birds. I hate to see them there, please be a darling and do something with them," and was angry with herself because she sounded weak and foolish. She was astounded by how different from her usual self she was being today. Even the phrase "be a darling" was alien to her. But, as she saw Jonathan walk away from her and back to the house, she thought that if sounding unlike herself was what was needed to keep Jonathan at bay she was willing to try it.

Everything was grey around her, the greyness that results from an absence of light, from too many sandy waves in the sea, too many clouds in the sky and at the earth's horizon. A dead greyness, she thought, not the live one of industrial urban environments. Though this was her weekend for rest and nature—and the last weekend on the rental contract of her summer share—she longed to be back in New York. Maybe it was because none of the friends she had shared the house with had decided to come to New Jersey this weekend: although they had repeatedly confirmed to her that no, it was too cold, too windy, too rainy, that they were sick and tired of that old piece of Jersey junk, she had hoped they would somehow change their minds. She shouldn't have hoped, she should have known better. Now she was stuck at an almost equidistant sixty miles from New York and Atlantic City with a lover she could not get rid of and two dead blackbirds. Enough to make me scream, she thought, enough to make me cry. Then she remembered something Barbara had said during a too hectic standing lunch of hot dogs on the corner of Wall Street and Maiden Lane: "Bond traders don't cry." She smiled at the memory, casting aside her unhappiness for a few nostalgic moments.

Why bond traders don't cry she would not have been able to say. That they were not *supposed to* cry was an obvious fact—it would have been an overt indication that they were too emotionally weak to withstand the pressures of their jobs. But don't bond traders sometimes cry anyway, in the privacy of their own rooms or in their best friend's arms? As far as she was concerned she was a damn good trader *and* cried a lot. She cried when she had to spend one more Friday night on her couch watching "Miami Vice" and eating microwave popcorn because some idiot date had decided she was dispensable; she cried at her friends' weddings when she felt her youth was running away too fast for her simply to hold on to it and play with life; she cried when she got home from work, found nothing to eat in the refrigerator and yet could not find any strength in herself for getting out of the house to shop; she cried when she was unable to fall asleep at night, tired and alone and holding on to the numbing promise of warm milk and Kahlua. Barbara had been wrong. As soon as she established this fact, the memory of the two of them, clad in grey business suits, huddled together under the yellow umbrella of the hot dog stand, lost its appeal and its comforting quality. She let tears flow and enjoyed their liberating wetness on her face.

She had reached the water's edge, and all around her were strands of stray grey seaweed, and unidentifiable pieces of plastic the storm had washed ashore (she noticed with revulsion the decapitated bald head of a doll, it was more pink than she ever remembered dolls to be), useless chips of broken seashells. Big white birds were screaming at her—cursing her for daring to intrude on their beach. Seagulls or albatrosses, she thought, and then added to herself, "And sincerely, my dear, I don't give a damn." A weekend on the Jersey shore with her lover and she had ended up on an empty beach talking to herself; it was a parody, life was making fun of her. Once more, as if on command, tears rolled down her cheeks and nose.

She never called Jonathan anything but a lover. Calling him boyfriend would have implied that for her he was more than just a marvelous love-making machine. Long ago she had decided not to call any man a boyfriend unless he was potential marriage material, and she had astounded herself with her old-fashioned decision. In the elation of her resolve she had almost wanted to call her mother and tell her that her daughter was—finally—considering marriage. Then she had realized it was all a farce, and that her mother would have too easily been able to see through it: a well-intentioned deception, well-meaning and righteous of course, but still not to be believed.

Yet, she also knew that Jonathan did think of her as his girlfriend, seriously considering himself as the male in a couple. A troubled couple, maybe, but one that would overcome the inevitable obstacles through hard work, compromises, and fighting. Compromises on her part mostly; fighting on his. So at least he seemed to think, though she had been the fighting one all along. Fighting *off* things, rather than simply fighting them. She fought off Jonathan's attachment, his vociferous closeness during the day and his sticky closeness at night, the frozen Japanese entrées he reheated for both of them at dinner (trusting that two pairs of laquered chopsticks on the table would provide an adequately elegant touch). She fought off his trite leftist (fashionably intellectual, he assumed) sermons, his invitations to revivals of unknown and unpronounceable German, Japanese, or Hungarian directors in cinemas down in the Village.

When she told him that she did not want to go out with him, that she preferred an evening at the Palladium to one at the Film Forum's Festival of Obscure Directors, he would act hurt and offended (although he should have known by now that her refusal would inevitably come). He is a nerd, she would say to herself, attempting to explain and catalogue Jonathan, he needs me so that he does not have to go to see movies and hear debates alone; without me he'd only feed himself on frozen food, without me he would sleep alone and *that,* I know, is no fun. At times she let herself be honest enough to add: and without him I would sleep alone too. She was not completely certain of this but she did not want to find out—the test might demand more loneliness than she was ready to withstand.

They had first met in the Guggenheim Museum, too distracted by the spiraling of Rothko canvases to notice that they were in each other's way. Jonathan's foot had crushed her own, his elbow dug into her side. "Will you still sue me if I get you a coffee?" he had asked and she had laughed, embarrassed by the physicality of the encounter, nervous because she should know better than to say Yes to a stranger in New York. "A coffee or I'll call my lawyer!" she had threatened him and thus put an end to her solitary afternoon at the museum.

For a while Jonathan's committed passion for what she

162

considered to be old-fashioned-sixtyish, bohemian issues had amused her. She felt intrigued by the immature youth that his unawareness of others' needs conveyed. After months of reluctant single nights, after sleeping uncomfortably alone for much too long (still on the left side of the bed because the right had been Richard's, and with not one but two pillows, side by side as if Richard had never left her), she was eager to hug Jonathan, tickled to be kissed by him. And after their first night she was surprised to discover that they matched in the rhythms of love-making, delighted because Jonathan had asked her what she wanted and had used his hand the way she liked, astonished almost to find that sex was once again a part of her. Jonathan's social naïveté and his erotic passionate courtesy made her feel like a child herself and for this she had been thankful.

She held on to him at first but then it was he who would not let go. He was sweet, caring, ever-giving. "A New York neurotic," she described him to Barbara, "hyper-intellectual and untogether. Sweet. Like all neurotics who one day come to realize that, if they want their girlfriends to last longer, they have to somehow compensate for their ways and shield themselves by piling up on sweetness."

She now felt indispensable to him, a need not masked but—rather—accentuated by his sweetness and by his open admission that he wanted to be with somebody, that he loved to spend time with her. He filled her space, all the time, every inch of it. Jonathan's presence, his phone calls and his politics, his love and need and devotion, weighted her. By now she was stronger and sated, and required him in small infrequent doses. But with Jonathan it was all or nothing and so, reluctantly, she had come to accept him, encumbered by his self-centered companionship, crushed by his blind altruism that did not recognize her. The summer had been a difficult one.

The walk on the beach reminded her of scenes from Film Forum movies—Lelouche's *Un Homme et une Femme*, Fellini's *Amarcord*, innumerable Bergmans and Viscontis, and the slow horizontal motions of Antonioni's camera. She saw herself as a stranger might see her, a lanky, long-haired woman proudly walking on a deserted beach, clouds and seemingly boiling ocean water and grey sand her only companions. She liked what she saw, mentally added "tears streaking her cheeks" to the description, smiled at herself, and walked on. She had saved herself for the day, she had fallen once again in love with the person that mattered in her life.

One white bird flew close to her, so close that his wings almost touched her face and she was able to hear their threatening flutter. Some bird! she said to herself, contemplating his loud and fast flight away from her, hearing his strident squawks progressively join and melt with the other beach noises. She remembered the birds on the porch, once again hoped that Jonathan had had the good sense to remove them; she really did not care anymore about performing a burial ceremony for them. Animal death seemed to be the perfect, natural response to a day like this: the weather itself would officiate in, sanctify, and notarize the birds' burial in the garbage can.

Yet there still was something that disturbed her in the birds' senseless death: they had come flying to her bedroom window during the storm because there, in her bedroom, they had seen light. She had insisted that Jonathan keep the light on, not out of any fear of the storm (as Jonathan seemed to have believed) but because—knowing that the torrential water would protect them from indiscreet neighbors' peeping —she had wanted to watch him and herself as they made love, had wanted to observe their joint action in each and every detail knowing that anything between her and Jonathan would soon become just a memory. Now she discovered that her curiosity had transformed itself into murderous voyeurism; she hoped that Jonathan would never understand this, that he would simply get rid of the birds without too much thinking about the real cause of their deaths.

She turned around, slowly walked back to the house. There was no choice but to go home: Jonathan was still pref-

164

erable to grey solitude. The sky had become darker, but it was fitting that it rain again, she thought. Looking in the distance she was surprised to notice how much she had walked, miles and miles, it seemed. She glanced at her watch, but 10:18 A.M. did not mean anything since she had no idea what time she had left the house. The long wet stretch of beach in front of her gave her the right to feel hungry and tired: as she walked—always slowly, leaving clean foot marks on the heavy sand—she dreamed of toasted English muffins dripping with butter and honey, freshly baked, piping hot blueberry muffins, waffles soaked with maple syrup, hot tea. All the while aware that she was preparing her mind and stomach for a certain delusion: there was almost nothing in the house by now. Most of the food had already been removed by people who had decided not to come this last weekend. For all intents and purposes she and Jonathan had been living in a closed house.

Living in a closed house was not new to her. In the kaleidoscope of the city, she had even come to cherish the centripetal comfort of closed spaces. The cinemas and theaters where she often spent her Manhattan evenings were closed houses, the top-and-bottom Medeco locks on her door assured that her apartment remain sealed to the unknown, double-pane windows preserved the airtight coziness of the trading floor. She had always liked the feeling of containment, in spaces as well as in human beings. She had discovered that the people she cared about were like drawings of living rooms in wintertime: a fireplace at the center, warm food and blankets all around, yet at the exterior—beyond the protection of the closed windows—they presented the bland chilliness of snow. But Jonathan was no comforting closed room anymore, and the house's isolated closure did not nurture but suffocated, strangled with clutches of coldness.

At the house Jonathan was nowhere to be seen, but the blackbirds were still on the front porch, their black feathers desperately moving in the fast wet air. She noticed that the feathers looked dull. Even the bright red of the blackbirds' blood had lost its color, it had been transformed into a crusty brown residue on the stone. She was furious with Jonathan, and felt she had every right to be. Now it was up to her to decide what to do with the carcasses. Waiting for Jonathan to come back was unthinkable: it would have granted him too much importance, shown him that he was more dear and necessary than he actually had the right to believe. Then she remembered that this was her next to last day in the house; the blackbirds could well remain on the porch, rotting on their own through the autumn rains and the winter snows. She walked into the house and tried to think of something else.

She had been right, the visions of muffins and scones dancing through her head had been just that, visions, not at all likely to transform themselves into reality. She plunged her hand into a tall box of corn flakes (an unsanitary habit from which she had never been weaned) and found them to be soggy, almost damp. Some idiot, she thought, some selfish idiot forgot to close the wax bag. As she methodically started opening the cupboards the first dull warnings of an oncoming headache developed in her temples. Lack of food, the usual cause of her many headaches. Every time she dieted she carried economy-size bottles of Tylenol in her purse, but now she had none as she had not thought of her Jersey summer share as dieters' territory. Hoping to prevent the headache she ran across the kitchen, opened the refrigerator, and removed two slices of whole wheat bread from the Pepperidge Farm plastic bag. As she ate them—almost ravenously, yet disliking every single bite—she thought that this breakfast was well suited to the whole weekend: hot waffles and pancakes just would have been misleading.

There was a glass percolator with leftover cold coffee at the bottom. Without warming the coffee she poured it into a mug and drank it, wincing because it tasted bitter. Bitter and greasy, and though its greasiness was unexpected and slightly suspect she found in it a confirmation of her weariness of Jonathan: leave it to him to screw up even drip coffee. She had not sat down yet, and her standing was as much an effort to reassure herself of the transiency of the morning (no day this disastrous could continue indefinitely) as a declaration of self-pity. She had so looked forward to a comforting Saturday brunch in a house by the shore, and was being punished instead with solitary cold coffee and limp bread in the kitchen. She worked so hard all week—trading foreign currency options, trading raunchy jokes, trading her feminist beliefs and sensitivity for the boys' approval at cocktail hour —and all she got in return were lousy weekends in fucking New Jersey! (Next year she would definitely get a share in the Hamptons.) She wanted love, but had ended up with somebody so needy for company that her only choice was to escape into solitude; she spent her weekend days running away from Jonathan, so that—after a hiatus of seclusion—she would be able to enjoy his closeness at night. How much is a night worth? she asked herself. And what about the two ravens (the two crows, magpies, blackbirds, those black *birds,* anyway) who were waiting for her to dispose of them properly, who had been the dual casualty of her kinky lust? How much is a night worth? she asked again but did not dare answer.

The wave of self-pity engulfed her, and before succumbing to its pull she tried to destroy it and break away from it by rationalizing. Maybe it's hormonal, she thought, but—as much as she believed in PMS's power—in all honesty it could not have been that: she was down to her last Tampax, had just had her period; she was still too young (thank god) for menopause, no way could she be pregnant, and it was unlikely that Jonathan could have been a biological variable—although she was sure that his very presence was sufficient to irritate her hormonal system and provoke in her endocrinological imbalances.

She climbed the stairs up to her bedroom. Jonathan was sleeping in her bed, naked, hugging *her* pillow in his arms. Anger overcame her sadness, and the anger took the form of an extreme proprietary feeling for her own pillow. She did not think that the pillow had only been rented, that it would stop being hers in less than twenty-four hours, that innumerable men and women had slept and slobbered, grunted and snored over it. She rushed to Jonathan's side and snatched the pillow from under his head. He awoke with a jolt and sharply asked her, "Hey you! What's wrong? You crazy or something?" She told Jonathan to get up, get dressed, and get rid of the magpies.

Jonathan still had not gotten up when she took off her own shirt and jeans and slipped into bed. After the cold coffee and the cold bread she was seeking the warmth of the blanket, she even appreciated the feeling of mild heat that Jonathan's body generated. She did not, however, appreciate Jonathan's body. She hissed, "Get out," because it was obvious that he was lingering in bed just waiting for her to join him. Although the way he lifted his eyebrows was a clear indication that he had heard her, he only moved closer to her, holding on to her arm, grabbing her like a child wanting a cuddle. A cuddle, she thought with annoyance and disgust, all I really need just now is a thirty-something-year-old grabbing me and getting ready to hug me and nuzzle my armpits. "The birds are *still* there," she meanly told Jonathan. "Fuck the birds!" he hissed at her. She was stunned by his reaction; even she, however, had to admit she deserved it. Even she, sometimes, was able to be honest about herself.

He put his hand over her shoulder, slid it down to her breast, cupped it so as to match the breast's convexity. She shrugged away from him, leaving his hand almost in mid-air. Moving further to her side of the bed would have meant losing out on the warmth; after her walk along the beach (and after her cold breakfast of cold coffee and cold bread, she would not let herself forget about that too easily) she felt she deserved warmth, she actually needed it. She decided to remain close to Jonathan, there were many ways other than physical distance to let him know that today she wanted nothing to do with him. At least, she reasoned, until he got rid of those black corpses. Thinking about them she shuddered and Jonathan—assuming that she was still cold—

pressed his warm body against hers and hugged her tightly. This time she was moved by his display of caring. She thought he would understand if she told him what she had been shuddering about and she said, "It's those dead birds, they give me the creeps—" He interrupted her, shouting, "What's wrong with you? Can't you think about anything but those birds?" and she thought that no, no, she really couldn't.

She did not answer. By now she understood too well that, for all his wide-eyed intellectualism and sweetness, Jonathan was egocentrically illiterate at reading her emotions and needs. At first she had attributed his limitations to typical male self-absorption and neurotic blindness. Yet soon (and without the benefit of an alternative theory), she had had to dismiss her explanation: Jonathan tried so hard to please her, was so sincerely eager to care for her and to be with her . . . and yet he never seemed to notice that she had so little time.

Maybe it was because—while she was charged with so many professional obligations, burdened by her managerial responsibilities—he was still an aspiring producer who supported himself through a succession of free-lance jobs that she barely recognized (copy editor, technician in a neuromagnetism lab, script reader). Jonathan had freedom and time and the day was his playground. Her days were busy, hectic— spent sitting and cursing in front of a green Wall Street monitor, eating take-out Korean salads and half portions of pasta with dried tomatoes and pignoli, calling from public phones to inquire if there were two grams of blow cheaply available anywhere in town (not using her own phone for illegal transactions was one more paranoid habit she had picked up as a teenager in her parents' home—only at the time it had been they and not the cops or a mythical vice squad she had been concerned with). She knew that hers and Jonathan's weekday worlds were so remote as to be practically inaccessible one to the other, that Jonathan bore no malice, that he could not know or understand. But this mattered little and, with increasing resentment, she felt herself becoming a prey to his demands and freedom.

Yet, occasionally, she still managed to be moved by his devotion, found her own self-worth confirmed in his myopic acceptance, clung to the anchor that Jonathan's presence provided. She wavered, uncomfortable on her emotional seesaw. And then there were the nights . . . Under sunlight, Jonathan could be boring, insensitive, an obsessive presence throughout, but moonglow transformed Jonathan into a lover, her magnificent love-making machine. Jonathan himself would have been quite surprised—maybe even flattered—had he known about the unsuspected male role he played in her life.

There were times when she hated herself for it all. For sleeping with a man she did not care about anymore; for not allowing him to see who she really was except when she told him she wanted to be alone; for the sin of omission she engaged in when she let him believe that she loved him; for having accepted the belief that lust triumphs over love. And in these moments she not only felt that she was debasing herself and debauching her own dignity, but that her transgression was much greater, almost cosmic. That her travesty of love perverted the very essence of being human, robbed her and Jonathan and anybody with whom she came in contact of their existence and meaning. An uneasiness close to panic rippled through her, and—though she tried to reason and reprimanded herself for giving way to absurdly illogical emotions—she would become certain that her deceptions betrayed nature itself, and that the aberrance of her actions challenged nature's laws and caused them to change.

Jonathan again tried to get close to her, and because she did not feel enough energy in herself to fight him off, she consented to let his body rest against hers. Still, she refused to talk to him, trusting that her silence would be a sufficient indication of her true feelings, fearing that—Jonathan being Jonathan, after all—it would not. "Those birds," he said to her in his usual sweet and pedantic tone, "why do you care so much about them? It happens every day, storms break out, birds become crazy and smash their heads against lit windows." So, she thought, even Jonathan had noticed the cause of the birds' death. The shared knowledge allowed her to feel less responsible for their deaths, less guilty about the light in the window. Grateful, she returned Jonathan's touch, let the memory of the morning's coldness glide away from her mind and momentarily substituted it with that of the bed's comforting effect. "Jonathan?" she asked, sliding her ankle along his leg. "Yesss?" he whispered in her ear and nibbled at her lobe. Her foot rested for a while above his knee. "Delicious ear," he commented and waited for her answer. But she was silent, slowly moving her foot up the thigh and toward his groin, so he said, "Oh, I love you too," and held her tight to calm the shiver that followed his words.

So she started going through the by now well-rehearsed motions of a love game interlude. The overture, touching Jonathan's body as if rediscovering it, although it had long since stopped holding any more secrets for her. Prolonging the overture to make sure that Jonathan would not fail in his duty to pretend to discover her own body anew. Pressing her lips over his nipples, tickling them with her tongue, nibbling them and sucking them. Letting him do the same to her own nipples, crying out in mock pain when he started biting them, allowing his hand to rest and move where it wanted— Jonathan knew very well what to do with his hands. Pressing her wet mouth and wet thigh against his own mouth and thigh, body matching body, parallel and one with Jonathan, holding her breath when he pushed hard against her. Between gasps she heard the window creaking, the glass pane clang as it endured the assault of the wind. She raised her head and saw the turbulent motion of clouds moving across the window. She heard her own syncopated breathing, the faint sloshing sounds of Jonathan's tongue working on her lubricated body, felt the tickling of his hair and the weight of his head as he moved it toward her stomach. She heard her own satisfied sigh, Jonathan gulp and whisper, "Sweet . . . oh my baby." She heard the long deep baying of the wind, the window frame rattle with dangerous metallic tones. And while she struggled to lift her head away from Jonathan's hold and check the frame, she heard the dull bang of two more birds flying against the window and cracking their skulls on the glass. By the time she had managed to free her head there were two identical lines of blood (both narrow, long, and very straight) streaking the glass pane with parallel red symmetry.

She cried out in terror and surprise, her body becoming rigid under Jonathan's hand. Jonathan, still unaware of what had happened, moaned with pleasure and she found his moan to be positively obscene. She jolted herself out of bed and ran to the window, working hard to open it while the wind invaded the room with motion and sound. On the front porch now lay four black forms: in the wind their feathers moved so furiously fast that she was unable to detect if all the birds were in fact dead. As if in mocking repetition, one more rivulet of deep red blood had formed near the small head of one of the birds. She started trembling with unknown fear and when Jonathan asked her what was wrong she was only able to whisper, "Come, come here," as if reality were too dangerous to allow her to talk in a normal voice.

Jonathan joined her near the window and both of them stood still in front of it, forgetful of their nakedness. "Strange," Jonathan commented, and then, in a typically rational fashion he explained it away. "I'm sure it's the low air pressure. Stupid birds hunt all those mosquitoes and flies and things buzzing close to the ground, and they become so enamored by the smorgasbord of insects that they forget about the houses and closed windows." He looked at her, noticing that his explanation had had no effect, that he had totally failed to reassure her. He tried to joke about it. "Two more ravens for the can—nevermore!" and she moved sharply away from him.

Today she felt absolutely alienated from everything that was happening to her, and especially from Jonathan. By now she was positively sure that there were no possible redeeming qualities to her weekend, and that the only option left to her was to pack up and get back to the city. Even nature had decided to turn against her, the dead birds were tragic and gory proof of the fact: and, as absurd as it all sounded to her urbane, sophisticated mind, she deeply believed it all.

And in the midst of everything that was happening, she did not even know what to do with her own body, so brutal had the interruption been. Pleasure had been snatched from her like a balloon tugging its own string and flying out of a child's hand, and, like a child, her body could not forget the object of its delight, contemplated its flight with the disappointment of unfulfilled promises. Jonathan closed the window, muttered, "Pretty disgusting," at the sight of the blood on the glass, and walked to the bed. "Don't be upset," he told her and when he sat down the mattress's movement was a gasp, not the bounce she had become accustomed to. "It's rather revolting but nothing more. Nature reveals itself red in tooth and claw in New Jersey." He chuckled, amused by his own wit. She was not amused but did not feel she had a choice; at that moment she even lacked the strength to pack her bags and leave. She grabbed Jonathan's brown sweater from the floor, wrapped it around her shoulders (away from Jonathan's warmth the room's chill was assaulting her body), and sat on the edge of the bed, right next to him. She did not even pull away from Jonathan when he made a motion to remove the sweater from her.

"Have you had any breakfast?" he inquired, as he placed the sweater on the blanket behind her. Worrying about her breakfast, here was his sweet and concerned self emerging again. But she became annoyed, if he had *really* cared about her breakfast he would not have been up in the room, sleeping, while she had had to eat refrigerated bread slices on her own. So she told him, "Yeah, I did," and though she injected in her voice as much sarcasm as she possibly could, he did not detect it. "Good," he said simply. She was left wondering if—through some mysterious transformation—Jonathan had also learned to be sarcastic, or whether his "good" had really been intended as such. Life, she sadly thought, was too complicated for her today.

Jonathan used her telling him that she had had breakfast

as an indication that she did not need anything anymore, that both of them were finally ready to spend a fun-filled undistracted Saturday in bed. Once again he placed his hand on her bare shoulders, pulling her toward him, but her body did not yield. She sat still and straight, unfocused eyes riveted on the glass pane. The blood was much more than just a testament to two birds' death; the marks' perfect vertical linearity, their sharp contours and their unfailing symmetry, created a pattern that she knew she was unable to read, had transformed the window into a symbol that she was too tired and confused to understand. In her mind she heard the muffled sound of the birds dying against her window, their croaking agony as they lay on the cold stone just under her room; in her ears she heard the furious cries of the seagulls as they circled above the ocean and the sand—up to now she had failed to take any notice of them. The cries sounded like a wail, a warning almost. She looked at Jonathan and pleaded with him, "Let's get out of here." "Don't be silly," he said, and with his hand he gave a squeeze to her shoulder. The seagulls, she thought, the seagulls are trying to tell us something and we don't know how to listen.

The seagulls, she thought, I don't even know if they are seagulls or albatrosses or big white doves. How can I then understand what they are saying? And the dead birds, she did not know what kind of birds they were either, she just knew they had died, in her territory. Suddenly knowing to what species they belonged mattered very much to her. She kicked aside the pretentions of urban ignorance and asked Jonathan, "What were they, the birds? Ravens or crows or what?" "*Still* those stupid birds!" he replied, angry and annoyed. "Can't you finally get those bloody animals out of your head? Or am I really such a turn-off today?" Bloody animals, he was right: there was no way she could forget that easily about blood on her doorstep and window. And, as for him being a turn-off today, he was right about that too, she thought.

She told him, "I'm still hungry," pulled her head and arms through the brown sweater and then, noticing it was shorter than she had expected it to be and that she looked pathetically and ridiculously erotic with her bare pubes and ass showing, she also put her jeans on. They were still wet and salty with ocean water, and she winced as she slid her legs into them. When Jonathan said, "I'm coming down with you, tell me what you'd like to eat," she thought, I could have stayed up here, in bed, but it was too late by now and, feeling the discomfort of the cold wet fabric against her thighs, she went down the stairs while Jonathan looked for his shorts and yet another sweater in her room.

The kitchen held less attraction for her than the front porch did. As she got ready to open the front door, she noticed that it had started to drizzle again, she heard the sound of thunder in the distance and then the sound of a second thunder, much closer to the house and to her. She pushed the door open using her strength, leaning against it. The cold front had arrived. The wind blew her long hair (her beautifully long hair) around, twisting the strands so that they coiled snakelike around her neck, they hit against her face, they blinded her by forcing themselves into her eyes. When she looked on the ground she noticed the blackbirds had not moved at all, strange since by the logic of things the wind should already have pushed them around quite a bit.

Their immobile presence seemed to have one single purpose, to engrave the birds in her mind and haunt her with their memory. She wanted to kick one of them, make sure that the bodies were indeed bodies, that they would move freely around, that *she* could move them freely around. That they hadn't—through an unknown yet by now not totally inconceivable process—glued themselves to the ground. Then it struck her that the coagulated blood could have functioned as a sort of glue, binding the birds to the pavement, and she laughed at herself for having been so irrational.

Once again she had to use all her force to open the front door. She left the birds behind her and, suddenly and unexpectedly grateful for the protection the house offered, she walked into the kitchen. In his shorts and T-shirt (she had

175

gotten hold of the only sweater he had brought along that weekend, and he had been too nice to complain to her about it) Jonathan was looking at the corn flakes box with a disconsolate look on his face. "They're wet," he announced. "I know," she sighed and for the first time this weekend both of them laughed together.

"They are bound to get wet anyway, as soon as you pour milk over them," Jonathan told her. "So go ahead, eat them," she answered curtly. He tried to appease her, took two lone eggs out of the refrigerator and asked, "How about some of these?" She remembered that the eggs had always been there, week after week and month after month throughout the whole summer, orphaned twin eggs nobody had ever wanted to break open. What concerned her was not the eggs' present state and probable inedibility: she worried that there must be something basically wicked or malignant about them—something everybody else in the house had known but which she had managed to ignore. Something that should lead her to avoid them, have Jonathan replace them in the refrigerator where they belonged. "Put them back," she told Jonathan and when he asked her why, she had to lie and tell him she didn't think they were fresh. "Time to throw them away, then, don't you think?" Jonathan said. No, she shook her head, no; she walked up to him, grabbed the eggs out of his hands, and gently placed them back on the shelf. "You okay?" he inquired, and she thought to herself no, I'm really cracking up. "Sure I'm okay, why?" she told Jonathan.

She eventually ate slightly charred toast sitting at the kitchen table side by side with Jonathan, her elbows touching his every time one of them lifted an arm to reach for the butter or jam. Not precisely her idea of a perfect brunch. But by now it was pouring, no chance of getting out of the house to take a walk by herself, and anyway, the sight of the dead birds had upset her so that she wanted—she craved and actively sought—normalcy.

She ate the third piece of toast and swore to Jonathan that if she kept this diet up, by the end of the day she would be transformed into a piece of starch. When he started to disagree — ready to launch himself into a convoluted explanation combining peasants' eating habits and carbohydrate digestion — she left the kitchen. If things were left up to him, Jonathan would have used hours upon hours trying to convince her of anything and nothing, talking endlessly just so that they would spend time together. Before leaving she sighed loudly, narrowed her lips, and twice raised her eyes to the ceiling: Jonathan could not remain unaware that his soliloquy had been the cause of her exit, would even possibly understand that she was tired of him, that he'd better leave her alone now that the summer was over.

She walked through all the empty rooms in the house, and in each room's musty smell she detected an official notice of summer's death and of autumn's assault. In the rooms' silence she heard the squeaking of loose boards, the rattling of windowpanes, the drumming of the rain across the walls and the glass. She noticed the scattered presence of abandoned T-shirts and bathing suits. Picking up a purple bikini top from the floor, she recognized it as hers, remembered she had unsuccessfully looked for it at the end of August, and wondered what it was doing in Anthony's room: she decided that she was probably better off not knowing.

Water was seeping through one of the windows in what had been Lisa's room. She watched the puddle that had already built on the floor, imperceptibly growing with every added drop that fell into it. When she looked out the window she noticed that the rain had formed a curtain between the house and the rest of the world: a thick lead colored curtain, almost a grey metal sheet, so impenetrable did it seem. The drops of water started to fall faster and faster on the floor and she heard thunder exploding with such deafening loudness that it seemed to be just above the house. Just *in* the house, actually. Unexpectedly, she felt glad not to be alone in it, grateful for Jonathan's annoying presence.

And then she became engulfed by a frightened homesickness for New York's Upper East Side, for the tidy, orderly familiarity of her apartment 15G (the seventh on a floor with nine similar apartments), for the MOMA or the Met where she would have spent a rainy afternoon. She did not want to touch the puddle on Lisa's floor, left the room while the water continued its rhythmic dripping through the window crack. Back in the kitchen she saw Jonathan using a slice of bread to sop up faded egg yolk from his plate: looking into the refrigerator she noticed it was empty, the two eggs were gone.

She was in a rage, but then again how could Jonathan have known? She had never told him that she did not want him to eat the eggs, she had failed to explain to him why they should not be touched. She had been embarrassed to make public her superstitious beliefs, and now she was suffering the consequences of her own cowardliness.

There was nothing she could really tell Jonathan and she thought, I need a break, and she thought, I need to take it easy, and she thought, I need a drink, I need one *now...*

A few leftover bottles—each holding a different residue of liquor or wine they had drunk and shared throughout the summer—were in the bottom shelf of a kitchen cabinet. Burrowing her head inside it she ransacked among the bottles and after much banging and clinking of glasses she finally pulled out a bottle of Bacardi, one of Gordon's gin (a September gift from Lisa's boyfriend), and three assorted bottles of cheap vodka. "So now you are gonna drink yourself stupid," commented Jonathan. He was still mad at the show of annoyance she had mounted on his behalf, at her leaving him alone in the kitchen. Jonathan did not often let himself become angry. Maybe, she thought, the mutual and exclusive proximity of this weekend not only exacerbated her need for independence, but also heightened Jonathan's sensitivity to her reactions, and sharpened his defenses. For a moment she considered that this could be interesting, maybe the hint of a new dynamic between the two of them, but she was weary, dulled and drained by the day's events, unprepared to accept any further changes or complexities. She saw Jonathan stare with condemnation at her bottles, looked at the yellow streaks of egg on his plate and, in a rage, she thrust the Bacardi in front of him and said, "Sure, got anything better to offer?" It almost disappointed her that he should not answer, it saddened her that, indeed, he did not have anything better to offer.

She mixed the rum with the orange juice she had bought on Friday at a New York deli—it had been one of the few items she had cared to take along for the weekend. When she finished the rum she continued with Screwdrivers and Jonathan joined her in emptying the carton of orange juice. They both had to drink the Gordon's straight, although she added some tap water to hers because she did not really care for the taste of gin.

It was lovely: the alcohol's warmth rushed through her veins, heating all of her limbs (like fire, she thought, aware that she was using a comfortable old cliché), burning her brain's neurons till there was little left, only a core that desired Jonathan, that imperiously demanded that he touch her like he had touched her before, an animal core that required he mount her and make her scream with pleasure. Once her intellectual critical barriers were down—she had already quite often remarked on this observation—Jonathan was wonderful regardless of what the time was.

Jonathan's neurons must have melted too, she thought, as she watched his hands moving in her direction. She tried to focus on his hands and was unable to, the fingers would never stay still and faded in a blurred wavy mass of brown pink. She looked at the bottles (three empty bottles, a residue of gin and a residue of vodka at the bottom of the other two) and though she desperately wanted to read the labels she could only distinguish one bottle from another by their shape. Before the kitchen started spinning, Jonathan's hands reached her, thrust themselves under her sweater (*his* sweater, to be exact), investigated the cavity of her belly button, made her tremble when they glided on the inguinal side of her thighs. She closed her eyes, and let her head hang backwards. Perfect bliss, she thought. Thank god for gin and vodka and that other stuff, she added.

She slid to the floor and Jonathan followed her there, actually helped her lower herself from the chair by sustaining her back with his hand, his arm muscles surprisingly strong considering how little he exercised. She lay on the wooden boards facing the ceiling, noticing that the lightbulb was dusty, that there were long spidery cracks in the grey ceiling, and that the cracks seemed to move as if in an attempt to knit themselves into a spider web. She closed her eyes once again to get rid of the weaving of the cracks and felt Jonathan's tongue lick her eyelids. Momentarily blinded, her hearing and tactile acuities reached a new peak: every time Jonathan's hands touched her she tingled, she felt the soft tickle of his hair against her face and chest, was able to imagine what his fingerprints looked like just by concentrating on the sensation that the fingers themselves provoked on her skin. She rolled over to exchange places, found herself over him, and then under him again, her legs constricted in their movements by the jeans that were wrapped around her ankles. Still keeping her eyes closed she blindly searched for Jonathan's ear to nuzzle, missed it because his whole body was moving much too fast, distinctly heard Jonathan's disorderly breathing, his hitting his shin against the table's leg, the patter of the rain against the house and on the ground surrounding it. She listened to the somber roll of thunder over the house, to the windowpanes rattle in a desperate defense against the wind; getting hold of Jonathan's ear, still trying to wrap her tongue around his squirming lobe she noticed that the whole house —she and Jonathan included—seemed to shake as if in a protest against the storm, that the thunder was so close to her that her own body resonated with its vibrations. She heard the rain turn into hail, the hail mix with new rain in a cacophony of aerial rage, the house's walls creak under the dual assault (she dug her teeth into Jonathan's shoulder biting him in her mindless frenzy), she heard the sound of a window breaking upstairs, the brittle sound of glass falling in one of the rooms and, soft among the unbearable clamor, she heard the sharp and distinct sound of two more birds hitting their heads against a window, smashing their bodies and cracking their skulls against the glass pane.

She screamed with the horror of known things, her scream almost a protest against the aberration that had just taken place, a refusal to recognize that nature's laws had changed for her and Jonathan. With a strength unknown to herself she levered her elbows against the floor and lifted Jonathan's body away from her. Her eyes now open she stared into Jonathan's and pleaded, "Let me go, let me get out," scrambled from under him and—having removed her humid jeans—she ran to the front door, opened it, exposing her naked heaving body to the fury of the skies.

By now she knew what she would find, and she was proved right. The birds were six, and new blood was pouring from two broken skulls, red immediately becoming pink as rain diluted it. One of the blackbirds had broken a wing in the impact of its death and—in its odd, twisted position— the wing now looked like the result of an unsuccessful attempt to attach an extraneous object to the bird's body. Unconscious of her nakedness, or perhaps not caring about it anymore, she bent her body and touched one of the bleeding birds with the tip of her index finger: it felt like a bird should feel, wet and slightly waxy, the feathers not as pliant as she had imagined them to be. She kneeled on the front porch and slid her finger across the bird's skull, discovering that the feathers on the top of its head were much softer than those on its body, that when she pressed the dented skull it gave way and her finger became covered with the bird's blood.

She heard Jonathan's annoyed voice calling her from the kitchen and she thought, how am I going to explain this to him? It seemed unfair that she should be the only one to be able to hear the birds' suicidal sound as they hit the house.

She walked back into the kitchen holding her hand up in the air, her finger dripping with the bird's blood. "Look!" she screamed at Jonathan. "It's happened again!" Jonathan grinned at her, "It's bound to happen during a storm—you look lovely . . . come here," he told her. In his grin she detected a conspiracy with whatever had led to the birds' death and she was sickened by it. She yelled, "Stay away!" when she saw him get up from the floor and approach her. She walked backwards as he came close, knowing that she was trapped between Jonathan and the front door, knowing that salvation lay nowhere around her.

It's madness, she frantically thought, it's the end. Jonathan reached her, placed his hands on her shoulders and his mouth on her bloody finger, asked her, "Where'd you get this blood, uh? What have you done?" I've done nothing, she thought—actually believing in what she was thinking—I've done nothing today, I have no cause, no reason in these killings, they're senseless, they're insane . . . She looked at Jonathan's naked limp body and wondered how she had ever been able to find warmth within it, comfort around it, how her desire could ever have been so blind. She tried to recall those moments and was unable to, she could only concentrate on Jonathan's red lips sucking her finger, match their color with that of the birds' blood, notice that they were an identical shade of crimson.

The birds, she thought, the birds, what were they? She enumerated, ravens and blackbirds and magpies and crows and starlings and black mutant albatrosses and freak seagulls and black doves . . . Nature had misrepresented itself, she had been betrayed by reality. Her chin was trembling, her chest was expanding and contracting fast just like it had expanded and contracted in the kitchen—but this time it moved out of fear and not out of pleasure. Jonathan's body leaned against hers, pushed it through the front door and once more she found herself on the porch, dead birds at her feet, standing still while Jonathan pressed his face between her breasts.

The sky looked as if it was about to collapse, draining itself of its rain in an effort to save itself from drowning. She felt the coldness of the water running down her face and chest, the liquid flow moving from her breasts to Jonathan's hair. She felt Jonathan's arms circle her, and she thought it does not matter, nothing matters anymore. She thought, it's

182

over and I never really wanted to know it. So she let her own head rest on Jonathan's, her own arms reciprocate Jonathan's tight embrace, her body mold into his, and—high above her head—she heard the dull thumping of bird after bird after bird heading straight into the glass of her bedroom window.

Alda, in Motion

When Alda smoked, he inhaled with very short, very nervous rasping sounds. That is, he would make a whole big production of it, just as he always did with everything else in his life. It bothered me, of course it bothered me, he and I sitting together in blue-tiled mirrored diners and Alda making all those sounds, coughing and clearing his phlegm-filled throat and rasping and letting everybody know we were there.

Other customers would lift their heads from their tuna fish sandwiches and stare shamefacedly at Alda and at me: they did not need to be polite because Alda was not. And they would stare even harder once they decided to at least try to identify what Alda was eating (always peanut butter-and-something sandwiches, disgusting combinations he alone would dare ordering). Waiters would also stare; the more expensive the diner the more condescending their looks, expressions of disbelief at Alda's sounds and food (peanut butter and marshmallow Fluff, peanut butter and sardines, peanut butter and orange marmalade, peanut butter and melted Velveeta, the whole messy thing always held together by untoasted soft white bread).

Alda's two hands grasping the sandwich, brown cream oozing from the sides, as he would repeat to me for the thousandth time that what he was holding was the most complete food available in our civilization. He eyed my Sunday morning eggs and bacon with distaste. And waiters would look at Alda in mockery, and customers would motion to the waiters to help them move their silverware and plates to a different table away from us as Alda ate through a cacophony of coughing and throat clearing. So, eventually, we stopped meeting on Sunday mornings; I had brunch uptown and never asked him where he went.

But, says Alda, there is such a thing as friendship, even if I don't understand what it's really all about. Me, that is, having lived all my life in Connecticut and New York, too spoiled and too selfish to appreciate the implications that a real friendship entails. This, at least, is what Alda says. While Alda himself is armed with love and passion, he is a real friend (once a friend always a friend), a person anybody can count on, even at three in the morning, always ready to come downstairs, ready for a trip to the bar and a drink. Again, that's how he sees himself. He is surprised and hurt when we see and treat him for what he is, an anachronism, a perennial big bear who will tag along with anyone who smiles and listens to him.

I had stopped meeting him for brunch, but he insisted we at least meet in the afternoon and so we did, usually in Central Park at the bench on the northeast corner of the reservoir. We would sit together, Alda and I looking at Manhattan across the blue mirage of the always still water; joggers sweating and panting as they passed in front of us in an orgy of Nike and Adidas and Alda rasping, smoking his Camels and coughing up pieces of his black lungs mixed with his tubercular spit. There they were, health and joggers and blue water and the Manhattan skyline, and I was spending my Sunday afternoons with a jerk who couldn't even stop coughing and who sometimes waited for me to join him before he would start eating his late brunch on a bench—Wonder Bread hiding peanut-butter-and-something, another of his unattractive (to say the least) mixtures. So, eventually, we stopped meeting on Sunday afternoons; I stubbornly jogged around the reservoir, two whole circles passing in front of Alda once every quarter of an hour. We would wave at each other and then I would head home to take a shower and play with the crossword puzzle. I don't know what Alda did on Sunday afternoons, and never asked him.

Laura asked, "What did you do to Alda? What did you tell him? He looks lost and sad. I saw him at Zabar's last Saturday," she says, "and he was sniffing Camemberts endlessly. Nothing else, I watched him from the Coffee Corner for *at least* fifteen minutes and he never moved from the cheese section, just stood in front of the Camemberts and smelled them all. Some kind of manager, the one with no hair and a long white coat, he never keeps it buttoned up, you know the one?" (No, I didn't.) "Well, anyway, he finally walked over to Alda and asked him if he wanted anything. And Alda—guess *what?*—he just walked away, like he did not owe any explanation or apology for having spent all that time touching and smelling Camemberts. Maybe he's having a breakdown," Laura said. I guess he was, but I could not concentrate on the issue. I kept on picturing in my mind Alda in his olive-green kitchen, broiling Camembert on top of peanut butter, and reflected on what it might taste like.

The summer was hot and sweaty, unused sheet crumpled at the bottom of my bed (no bedspread, of course), summer perspiration being soaked up directly by the musty mattress. The air carried the weight of diesel oil, fried chicken and

Szechuan Empire oil, Coppertone oil, all trapped and fermenting under the heavy curtain of the New York sky. Whether it was night or day did not matter: the city always smelled the same. Only thunderstorms would wash the smell away for an hour or so, too short a respite to really make any difference at all in my life. So when the phone rang I woke up and out of my sweat (it was 2:20 A.M.) and it was Alda on the line wanting to know where I had been and how I was. I just wanted to go back to my dreamless nocturnal sauna, I told him he was an imbecile (calling me at this time of night!) and hung up. I wish I could say that I spent the rest of the night in sleepless remorse, but the truth of the matter is that heat always leaves me groggy-tired and lazy, so I actually slept quite well until my alarm rang and I got ready to brush my teeth and wipe off the heat of the night with the morning shower.

I don't know how he ever came to be called Alda: I don't *think* that's his real name, and I *know* it's not his last name. I asked him about it once and he was, as usual, very vague about it. He told me his father's name was Luciano and his mother's was also some other foreign name I now can't remember. But he did not tell me anything about his *own* name. Once again I knew of Alda only and just exactly what he wanted me to know. Which constantly leaves me wondering about him, maybe he is a terrorist in hiding, or maybe a leftover from the radical sixties, or maybe I am just making too much out of too little, and he is just a sweet man who does not have it all together, with a few loose neurons in that big brain of his. He is the older version of what we have all left behind.

I knew the likes of him in my college days. I was one of them. Then we had shared joints, cheap red wine, and solemn promises of never-ending friendship. We had marched together in Washington, painted each other's cardboard signs, lifted our hands to make the peace sign when we met in front of the library. We were the children of a time that did not want us, and we and the time were proud of our mutual rejection.

Then my hair had been as long as Anthony's, and in the morning we had stood naked in front of the mirror and braided each other's uncut manes. There had been Anthony and Sarah and John and Elizabeth, but soon we had invented new names for ourselves—Dylan, Sunshine, Zonker, Aretha —to reinforce the establishment of our new identities. We had shared food and drugs and dreams, had sworn we would never sell out and become the establishment. John and Sarah would be poets and join Allen Ginsberg in his meditative chants, Elizabeth would teach art to Appalachian children, Anthony would fight the Vietnam War from beyond the Canadian border. Now John is a copywriter for Camel cigarettes, Sarah plays with junk bonds which she insists on calling "high-yield securities," Elizabeth teaches at a private though progressive elementary school in the Village, Anthony got married for the third time before giving up on married life for good and moving to Edmonton, Alberta. And I graduated, and two years later I cut my hair and my parents promised they would not only pay for law school but also support me through the coming three years. We all had had to say goodbye to our childish, crazy beauty. I don't know that Alda ever did.

Alda and I first met at one of those pompous gallery openings in SoHo, cheap white wine with ice cubes melting fast in plastic cups, expensive oversized or overtight dresses, and air-conditioning systems that never work. I say "we met" when I should really say "he met me" since I was busy flirting with a twenty-year-old tanned beauty, not expecting to get anything out of my efforts but a confirmation that he was gay, as I already suspected. He was, but he did not let me know until the end, enjoying too much the pleasure of my admiration, but that is another story.

Alda, the bear, stopped just in front of my blond Greek Kouros, and without even looking at him asked me did I like the paintings that evening and would I come have dinner with him? I did not like the paintings, typical red spaghetti that sells as post-Pollock in New York, and I was pretty hard up financially at the time (I still am, but now I sublet my bedroom when things get too tight) so I accepted. What the hell, if necessary I could always find some way to escape before dessert.

It was not necessary, especially because he did not even offer me any dessert. Now I know that his sandwiches provide him with an all-in-one meal, dessert included; some women's diets do just the same, pouring liver and eggs and bananas and milk in the blender and mercilessly swallowing the liquid punishment. But Alda *chose* to eat the way he did, did not seem at all embarrassed by it that evening. So at the Ear Inn I ordered quiche (safe, noncommittal choice), but he asked for a BLT with peanut butter on white. And I stared and stared while he took huge bites out of his sandwich and with Crayolas drew hearts for me on the paper tablecloth.

That's another endearing trait of Alda. He does not know the way he looks (doing what he is doing, dressing the way he dresses), and he does not care about it either. Drawing hearts while a combination of bacon grease and peanut butter dripped down on his chin, holding the pink Crayola with one hand and the BLT with the other, not even bothering to put it down on the plate between bites. He drew hearts and pyramids and cats' faces and then took the subway home while I paid for a cab (he lived on the West Side and I lived on the East).

He called me later that very same evening to ask me if I wanted to see him again. I of course told him that I would call him back in a couple of weeks, but then I got this invitation for a long weekend on a sailboat near Chesapeake Bay, and then another long weekend at a bed and breakfast in Woodstock, and me and Andy only thought about each other for two short and lust-filled months, so Alda fled from my mind, becoming only a greasy downtown memory.

And after Andy, I needed to go away from New York to

recuperate so Laura and I pooled some money together and fled to Europe. When I came back there were thirteen phone messages from Alda on my machine. I was annoyed (of course I was, the tape had even run on to the very end leaving no space for any further messages, and had it not been for Alda's stupid and long hellos this might not have happened), but Laura said we *must* call him, it was just too funny. So we called him together and he invited us both to share a sandwich with him in Central Park. This is *precisely* what he said: "Share a sandwich with me." As if he had been speaking about Dom Perrignon or coke. Laura said we *must* see him, it was just too weird, who was this man *anyway?* So we met him in Central Park, and Alda brought along Wonder Bread and baguettes, crunchy Jiff and tinned brie and jarred pimientos to make sandwiches with. Laura and I almost collapsed laughing, but he was really a very sweet man, undemanding and sweet that is, so I started meeting him more and more often, started noticing how he coughed and smoked, his yellowed fingers with thick black-tipped fingernails.

Alda wrote poems and neverending letters in his studio on the Upper West Side, then he moved to Chelsea (he said that just walking in front of the Chelsea Hotel inspired him) and took his basset hound, Edmund, his books, and his futon along. He then moved two blocks west, near the Roxy, and throughout the night his whole apartment would reverberate with bass rap sounds and stomping feet. He could not sleep, and when he would finally doze off at three in the morning Harleys burning the asphalt on Nineteenth Street would jolt him wide awake again. So Alda moved once more in his desperate and futile search for an affordable and livable apartment in New York. He disliked roaches (who are notoriously very fond of open jars of peanut butter) and he disliked motorbikes, rap sounds, drunken bums in front of his door, all abundantly found on Nineteenth Street. And Alda moved again, closer to me this time, always with his books and his dirty dog, leaving his futon behind because at the time he was subletting a so-called furnished studio and he had no room to put the futon in.

So Alda moved and Alda moved, always calling on me to help him, asking me to take care of his smelly dog till he found a building that accepted pets, depositing copies of old Delmore Schwartz books in my bookshelves and taking them back just when I was beginning to get interested in them, leaving baggies of dope for me to watch over while he ironed out the last details of the deal. And me, naïve and stupid like I never had been since the days I called myself "Rainbow" and like I never will be again, me actually *nursing* his ridiculous dope, making sure the baggies did not get too warm, fearing that one day the cops would break in and arrest me as an accomplice.

I told him I did not want to be the guardian of his dope and he was hurt but I can't say he understood. Uninvited, he sat on my couch and let the ash on his Camel get longer and more tilted so that I had to focus on the ash and worry whether it was going to fall on the floor or on the couch rather than listen to what he was telling me. The ash finally fell on the floor but that did not make a difference, I still had not heard Alda's explanations and I would remain oblivious as to *why* I was needed to take care of him, of his dog, and of his dope.

Alda found a new apartment, a terrible pad in a terrible neighborhood, junkies and Puerto Ricans blasting their boxes at any hour of the day and the night. He would have done much better for himself had he just stayed in the studio near the Roxy, but it would have been useless to try to explain something like this to a person as stubborn and weird as Alda.

Laura says she does not understand what I see in Alda. I rather think that the problem is: what does Alda see in me? He could be wasting his time with other friends who do know what friendship means. Wasting, I say, and not spending his time, because Alda flutters around me like a moth, not taking anything *in,* not evolving or even just changing. He still eats the same foods he did when we first met in SoHo, he changes apartments once a month or so, and he sits in Central Park (folds of stomach fat resting on his thighs like rolled carpets) and watches urban joggers, vicariously building a sweat by moving his neck to follow them.

I asked him once. I said, Alda, do you like it here in New York, wouldn't you be better off someplace quieter, someplace like Maine or Vermont where there are no roaches or seven-hundred-dollars-a-month studios, or ghetto boxes? You could even find a house there, a real place for yourself and Edmund. Seemingly I had offended Alda, implying that he was not strong enough to survive in a Darwinian city like New York where only the fittest can thrive. He sulked and said time and time again, Oh well, if you want me out of your life just say so... He also mumbled indignant words into Edmund's ear, something to do with not *even* being understood by the people who were supposed to be his friends. So I let the matter rest, I am no fool and can tell when my suggestions are not wanted.

Alda called me up and said he thought he had cancer. He was coughing more than ever and his lungs hurt even when he did not cough. I had been taking a shower, and now I was standing with the phone receiver near my ear, licks of shampoo foam in my hair, dripping wet on *The New York Times* scattered around my desk. Drying fast in the humid but hot summer air I told him I would call him back soon, as soon as I finished rinsing, and stepped back into the shower crying.

Then Laura called and asked whether I had heard the news, and once again I was dripping on the by-now-unreadable and sodden *Times* science section. Laura would not cry at this kind of news or, at least, she would not start crying *right away* like I do; so I blew my nose in the towel, tried to keep an unemotional, uninvolved, and so-what's-new voice, all the while hearing Laura's details about black lungs spitting blood and had she ever told me about her mother's cancerous ovaries?

While drying myself (more out of habit than necessity) I got on the phone to Marc, arranged to have Alda visit him at Sloan-Kettering, briefed him about Alda's lack of funds and how wonderful Alda was. Three days later Marc and I met for cocktails on his terrace, and looking at the orange hazy sunset through scattered watertanks, Marc told me that Alda was as healthy as anybody could hope to be, he was just too fat and smoked too much for his own good. Many men, said Marc, need attention and fabricate little medical lies to get it. Many women do the same, Marc added.

I was so furious I called Alda straight then and there, from Marc's apartment, and yelled at him over the phone. Alda seemed genuinely surprised by my anger; maybe he expected me to be overjoyed by the news of his instant recovery from lung cancer, I don't know. I told him if those were the games he played I simply did not want anything to do with him anymore, and hung up. Alda sent me a big basket of weeds with some flowers in between (mostly weeds, but it *still* must have cost him quite a bit), asking for forgiveness in the most traditional way. I waited four days before I called him again to ask him meanly how his lungs were. He did not detect the irony and said, Very well, thank you.

We were sitting sharing popcorn in a movie theatre on Bleecker Street, watching *The Wild Child* by Truffaut. Alda dipped his hand into the popcorn carton at least five times as frequently as I did. I stared at the screen, and he stared at the popcorn. I finally told him that pigging out on popcorn that way was gross. In the movie theatre's silver darkness Alda's eyes shone and looked very sad. Alda did not eat any more popcorn and I did not feel I could eat any either. We punished each other and the kernels grew cold and soggy with oil in the waxed paper container. At the exit I wanted to throw the

always looking at Manhattan through the Hudson and dreaming of being there . . .) Laura says Ithaca might do him a lot of good. When I finally asked him why he wanted to go Alda told me he did not have enough space in New York. And maybe he *will* like it in Ithaca, maybe he will live with people that like to watch just like he does, maybe he will meet birdwatchers and starwatchers (they say the skies are incredibly clear up north) and organic people who like watching things grow in organic shit. I said, Go, you might like it up there.

I have not seen Alda for four months now. I know that he is in Ithaca standing still in supermarkets hoping to catch a whiff off the Cheez Whiz jars, marveling at the friendliness of upstate squirrels. But Laura said she saw Alda at Leo Castelli two nights ago and he was staring at a Clemente bottle —green canvas with a wheel in the corner. I did not believe her, but if what she says is true, I know that that wheel spun and rolled and moved faster than Alda did.

Slow Train Coming

The Puerto Rican girl sitting across from me is drinking Pepsi and eating Fritos. She plunges her hand methodically into the bag, eats a chip, and takes a sip of the cola. If people are going to eat this kind of total junk they might as well enjoy it, but she doesn't. She looks serious, eats Fritos and drinks Pepsi to survive, just like children eat bologna sandwiches and Campbell's soup at lunchtime. She looks young enough to still be in school, has acne pimples, a fat stomach, and tight-fitting no-label jeans. She is probably pregnant and right away I want to tell her that she is already, much too soon, doing terrible things to her baby, eating all that junk and adding caffeine in the bargain. But it's none of my business, is it?

The subway is stuck between two stations and indistinguishable announcements are being yelled through the train's sound system.

At my right sits a woman with a grey fur coat. Beaver, I think. Coyote, muskrat, I think. Chinchilla, maybe. She looks bored, nibbles her nails, removes her finger from her mouth for a couple of seconds and then sticks it back again. It's incongruous, she's much too elegant to eat her nails: I notice the red polish on them, recently applied. I know, because it still looks perfect, it covers all the nail, up to the edge. I want to tell her, don't eat your nails, you'll spoil your looks, you're so perfect now . . . Sometimes, really, I'm worse than my mother.

At my left an old man, he's staring into space though he's carrying the *Post* folded on his knees. It's Wednesday, the food section day, and I'd like to ask him if I could have a look at the paper. But you don't talk to strangers—first—and, second, the *Post* has probably been recycled from a garbage can, he's a poor old black man after all. It's not as if I were afraid of germs, but garbage cans in New York are disgusting. Riding in the subway you get the feeling that the garbage has overflowed from its cans, seeped underground into the cars and finally rested there.

The Puerto Rican teenager throws the empty plastic Fritos bag on the floor. She keeps the empty Pepsi can in her hand: she can redeem it for five cents after the ride is over.

I don't have a boyfriend in this city. I have a lover, sometimes I have more than one, but they all smell the same to me. In the morning their armpits carry the pungency of ripe male sweat, their backs are sweetly moist and sticky, and only a whiff of my own juices remains on their warm limp cocks. I haven't made love in three weeks and tonight I'm supposed to see Cliff on West Ninety-seventh Street. By tomorrow—if this subway doesn't move—I won't have made love in three weeks and one day.

Cliff and I don't really know each other. We met in a SoHo loft at a networking party of a friend of ours. Networking parties have become very popular: there is no need to serve any real food, no need to work at making sure there will be a diverse crowd (inviting all under-forty professionals in three related companies seems to be a favorite option), and the quality of the music does not matter—who wants to dance with business-suited red-tied investment bankers anyway? I never thought I would meet anybody interesting at a networking party and I might still be right. After all I still really do not know Cliff.

He's good looking, he's certainly got that going for him. Not too tall but almost Nordic, built in a rectangular solid shape with ash blond hair. He is, I think, the kind of man who would not mind if I clung to him and bit him throughout a whole sleepless cocaine night. Three weeks ago Gregory told me he could not take it anymore.

Hold him and wrap my tanned arms around his chest *if* this subway will move, that is. Or we might be stuck here throughout the night. For all I know Cliff might be riding this same train, sweating under his Brooks Brothers uniform. For all I know I could go looking for him, lose my seat, and spend the rest of the night leaning my back against a closed subway car door. If the wait keeps up for long I won't even bother going to Cliff's place. I drink much better on my own anyway. I sleep—when I sleep, if I sleep—much better on my own too.

How did the Puerto Rican teenager know she should take the Fritos and the Pepsi along with her in the car? I'm not hungry, but I'd give anything for chips or pretzels or a drink. I never eat because I'm hungry, I only eat because I'm nervous.

If Cliff has taken an earlier train he must already be home. He is the kind of man who'd have champagne in his refrigerator, waiting for me. Good thing champagne is not like wine, you don't have to uncork it and let it breathe. Otherwise, Cliff's champagne would have been flat by now.

If the old man on my left at least opened his stupid paper I could peek and discreetly read along. Though I know myself by now: I always read much faster than anybody who is a *Post* reader. Then I become impatient—why don't they turn the page, how fucking long can it possibly take to pruriently scavenge through Ann Landers's column?—snort at them, stop being a clandestine reader and become an intruder in their pathetically limited information field. Sometimes they even get up and leave. A woman once threw her *Daily News* in my lap and walked away. But she seemed slightly deranged and, anyway, she got off at the next stop; she had only used me as a convenient trash can.

I have nothing to read in my briefcase. It's unusual and, of course, it had to be today. I generally carry a book with me in the subway. Sometimes I carry a whole stack of *Vogue* and *Elle* and *W* magazines. I even work underground. Cliff says this is neurotically endearing; he understands me better than so many of the boys and men I knew in the past who pretended to know me as well. Cliff would not want me to be what I am not, nor would he ask me to give up on what I want to do just because he has other plans in mind.

The conductor's voice is supposed to give information and reassure the passengers. But the car's intercom is blasting pure nonsense. There are only two choices: let the decibels hurt your ears, or let the decibels hurt your ears and your head as you try to understand what is being communicated. Nobody, it seems, has chosen the latter option. When I was young I was always told that if I got lost I should ask a policeman for help. I got lost, but the policeman could not understand what I was telling him through my blubbering sobs. He took me to the police station where in frozen terror I sucked lollipops for four straight hours; two policemen kept on smiling at me and asking me questions I could not answer because I wanted to go to the bathroom so badly and didn't dare say so. When my mother finally stepped into the police station (she herself had called the police, denouncing my disappearance as a kidnapping) my joy at seeing her overflowed: I wet my pants and the yellow puddle drenched the desk I was sitting on. I had—my mother told me when I was older —gotten lost one block from my home; the bagel shop had closed and a new **AU PETIT PAIN** sign that I did not recognize had been put in its place.

Everybody says aaahhh . . . The subway has moved half a yard jolting all passengers out of balance, West Side people fall onto Wall Street people but nobody seems to mind. Had we only tried to understand what the conductor was saying we would have been warned, and we are moving, aren't we? No, we are not. It was just an underground whim, the stupid thrashing around of an agonized beast. I think, the subway is like a millipede losing its legs one by one (how many years would that take?). I think, maybe they've given up on this subway, in a year in New York how many people are left to be asphyxiated in closed subway cars parked on secret rails? I think, maybe Cliff has given up on me, I've certainly given up on him by now. I wonder if I can sue the MTA for ruining my sex life.

Nobody will ever know that a train full of passengers has died on its subway tracks. Nobody will be able to mourn for us. The comforting thing about funerals is that they are the only insurance we have that we will be remembered—however briefly—after we are dead. But if I die in this subway they won't even know where to look for my body. No matter what anyone says about the worthlessness of the body, a funeral without a body just isn't a funeral. Remembering is not enough, in my life and death I need the reassurance of tangibles.

Cliff will say, "I didn't even get to meet her, she didn't give me a chance." But, I must say, maybe it's better this way, twenty-nine is so dangerously close to thirty. . . . I had promised myself that I would stop having lovers and start having boyfriends when I turned thirty: maybe I can start practicing my good resolutions at twenty-nine, though there's nobody in my life who could even remotely qualify as a potential boyfriend. Freedom lies with lovers, after all.

The subway gives another jolt but does not even move half a yard this time.

I do many things well; I will get a promotion in two

weeks, I was told informally; it will be the second promotion this year. I have this uncanny ability of knowing when to yell at models and buyers and when to pamper them and still get them to do what I want. I cook well, when I have the time: cold Chinese noodles with peanut sauce and Italian spaghetti with fresh pesto (I use pignoli, not walnuts) and soba in a black Miso broth redolent with vegetables; I seldom eat what I cook, though, but nibble on cold leftovers on the following days. I am a good lover, I play with my lovers and with myself, tease them and leave them in the middle of their passion only to start again when they cannot stand it anymore. My body is pliant and I love inventing, let my ideas take the form they want and translate it through my body. I have fun and never demand conversation over breakfast.

I do many things well, but waiting in the subway is not one of them. I think, I am the kind of person who'd rather be run over by a car than wait at a red light.

The old man has fallen asleep. His neck has lost its tonus, chin resting on the chest and his mouth is slightly open. He breathes and a disgusting, ranting noise rolls out of his throat. It's as if decades of dried up mucus had decided to come loose in him tonight. At his every rant his germs creep on me, leave him to enter my body. I want to throw up, I want to leave, but I remain sitting, waiting, looking down at my hands and at my electric blue pumps. I must be losing my mind.

The Puerto Rican teenager puts the can of Pepsi near her feet, picks up her discarded Fritos bag from the floor and examines it. She reads the ingredients and I think that, now that she knows, she won't buy this shit anymore. But I don't believe it, I know she will continue eating Fritos until her ass becomes too wide for size-sixteen jeans and Puerto Rican men will stop saying *"Qué linda mamacita"* when she walks down Fourteenth Street. Then she'll say to herself *Por qué? Por qué? No soy linda?* but it'll be too late, there is no way back from a size sixteen.

From my left, buried beneath the beaver fur, the red-nailed woman's voice addresses me. "Is this . . . common?" she asks, and I say to her, "You're from Louisiana, are you not?" She says, "My god yes! now if that isn't just something, well howd'ya ever know?" and I want to tell her, look sweetheart, you sound more Dixie than Scarlett O'Hara ever did, but for the first time since I have noticed her she looks passably calm and happy—not nibbling/sucking her finger anymore. I don't want to spoil her newly found nirvana and I simply tell her that there's something in her speech that reminds me of people I know in New Orleans. A lie, of course.

So she talks and talks and I openly ignore her, try very hard not to listen to what she's telling me. Something about New Orleans, I'm sure; maybe I'm missing the perfect recipe for Cajun blackfish right now, but today I don't want to hear the noises of the subway, not even the civilized ones. Eventually the chatter at my right stops: I hope she's not too offended—but I don't mind if she is. If she's likely to go back to her native Dixieland and tell everybody how unfriendly New Yorkers are. Me, I'm one of them, of course.

Not unfriendly, maybe, just savvy and aware. Strangers are strangers, the subway is never safe even when stuck in tunnels. *Especially* when stuck in tunnels. Giving my mind the empty space to think, the challenge of decisions, should I take the train back home, call Cliff (and, if so, do I apologize for being late?), go straight to Cliff's apartment? Throw my briefcase on his floor, hug him and whisper into his neck, Cliff it was horrible . . . Tell him I never thought I would make it out alive, I hate the subway, from now on it's cabs or nothing for me. Probably nothing.

Because, after tonight is over, it will be a long time before I take a cab to go to Cliff's. We won't see each other for days, weeks. It's the freedom of lovers, of the occasional lovers in my life: and occasional can mean "often" just as easily as "almost never." For me it means the latter: "occasional" is random, infrequent, "occasional" is wild and impulsive. "Often" is a promise, a tie to one another. "Often" overflows its boundaries, my boundaries, robs me of my

205

space. The space I wanted Cliff to fill tonight. The space which—right now, in this car—the Metropolitan Transit Authority of the City of New York is denying me.

She talks and talks, the furred, red-nail-painted, well-dressed Louisiana woman at my right, talks though I am not looking at her, though I try hard not to acknowledge her presence anymore. She talks and, if she weren't so well dressed, her incessant babbling would qualify her as one more deranged homeless woman talking to herself while roaming the New York subways. Maybe she was specifically hired by some demented N.Y.U. social psychology professor with an NIMH grant to test frustration levels in overcrowded, forced confinement settings. And, as the MTA is undoubtedly sponsoring the study, some part of my one dollar subway fare must be tax deductible.

I disgust myself: the innumerable stupidities I resort to thinking about . . . they spring and then reside in my head just to keep me from becoming utterly paranoid and freaking out. Just to keep other passengers' voices in the background (though I am having *some* trouble with the woman at my right), to convince myself that there must be some logic to the situation—and therefore an eventual end to it. Maybe I am a closet claustrophobic. Or is that an oxymoron?

The Puerto Rican teenager speaks. Wails, rather, lets out a rotund, bored moan *"maaadre de diiio . . ."* The orange Fritos bag is still in her hand. The can of Pepsi is still near her feet: it has not yet rolled across the car in its inevitable mission to release the last drops of flat Pepsi cum saliva on somebody's seventy-five-dollar Italian shoes. The girl fidgets, twists the Fritos bag so that it produces crumpling noises.

Cliff told me that he had worked at a pizza restaurant when he was at Cornell. They served no drinks, it was a cheap-paper-plates and vegetable-oil-mozzarella joint. He bussed tables, shredded the plasticky mozzarella and made sure the glass jars were always full of garlic salt, oregano, and red pepper flakes. The garlic salt and the oregano came in big paper bags and from those he filled the jars, first thing in the morning. All the jars sat on a back table and, if he spilled some oregano or garlic powder he would have to scoop it back in by wiping the table with the side of his hand. During the whole first term of his sophomore year his hands smelled of garlic. He was aware of their smell even when he was asleep, and never had the courage to approach any girl for fear that he'd be told he stank. He already knew he stank but did not want to be reminded of it. In March he was taking a hot shower and the steam was heavy with the pungency of garlic powder. His body had started to smell like his hands. Cliff left the pizza joint and got a work-study job feeding hairless mice in biochemistry labs. This is why Cliff never cares to have a pizza even if he hasn't eaten anything all day and is probably quite hungry. This much I know about Cliff. I really don't know much more.

But I do, I do. I know Martha, his last girlfriend, left him because she felt constantly uncomfortable, threatened by his need for order and precision. So Cliff says, but then she must really not have known him; Cliff might be rigid in his life, but to others he offers the choices of either ordered precision or the chaos of freedom. One night Cliff talked about Martha. He said, "She was a photographer and used the world like a camera field. She only bothered to respond to it when the light was right, when the people were set in front of her and looked at her the way they were supposed to. She only wanted to become awake when her eyes held the right color filters, but I could never tell which color it would be, when it would be needed, what would be required from me. Why she wanted me." You can't love a person unless you know what you want from him and why it's him that you want. I seldom know, of course.

Cliff loves the fact that I am undemanding, has told me so himself. He does not, however, love *me* because I am undemanding. He loves "the fact" instead. It is precisely because I ask little from him, because I make sure we remain independent from each other and do not burden each other with demands of commitment and responsibility, that he does not have to love me for what I offer him. What I offer is the negation of a real offering. You don't love somebody because she gives you nothing.

Cliff is somewhere on West Ninety-seventh Street waiting for me in his one bedroom on the third floor. Yet his waiting means that I am placing demands on him; spare your time for me, Cliff babe, give me your time even when I am not around you, even when you can't see me and feel me. Wait for me, don't dare call anybody else till I come into your apartment. Keep your evening empty, filled only by the possibility that I might still appear at your doorstep. It's getting late, it's very hot in this subway car. . .

"*Maaadre de diiio . . .*" the Puerto Rican girl moans again. The Louisiana woman near me has stopped her gabbling and is busy fanning herself with a *New York* magazine. The air movement reaches my right cheek and it feels good, though I childishly feel I don't deserve it. She is doing all the fanning and I was not very civil to her a while ago. But I brought no magazines along today, I have nothing to fan myself with. So I steal her air, take advantage of her efforts. Somebody from the end of the car yells, "What's wrong with these motherfuckin' trains?" and many people bother to come up with an answer.

It jolts. It moves. It sighs. It rests. It jolts again but this time — rendered savvier by the previous failed attempts — nobody says anything, there are no more shrieks of anticipation and weary delight. It moves slowly, like an injured animal, and in the car we are all united in silence, holding our breath to see if it can make it. Silence in a subway car at rush hour: it's creepy and abnormal; it's sick. It is as if we were a convoy of contagious people, an infected human load plagued with typhus, smallpox, AIDS . . . The train slows down and stops and coughs and spits and resumes its march and inside its cars we are all waiting, coughing and spitting and holding our breath with it. The woman at my right has placed her little finger back into her mouth. She is not only sucking her nail now. She is biting down on it, hard.

It creeps on its tracks, wheezes in its effort, each wheel rotation a distinct muffled metallic sound. Muffled and metallic. Metallic and muffled. It sounds like "clanff" or "cliff." Cliff... Cliff... Cliff... It is too absurdly easy to assign our own meaning to the nonsense that fills our lives. The wheels move slowly and say Cliff... Cliff... Cliff... and, no matter how hard I try, I cannot get rid of their voice in my head.

The woman from Louisiana asks me, "Excuse me, but do you have *any* idea of how much longer the ride will last?" and though I am dying to give her a sarcastic reply I tell her, "No, really not, I'm sorry," and so I repay her for the fanning.

It moves, it moves, and on the walls of the subway tunnel appears a faint watercolor of grey-yellow light, the station ahead. We are all silent as the train—tired, slow, dying—pulls into the station. In an almost ominous calm, in an unprecedented and thus menacing order, we march out of the train, form a double line climbing up the stairs to Seventy-second Street, walk out into the hot streetlighted New York night.

A taxi takes me to Ninety-seventh Street but nobody answers when I buzz Cliff's apartment. So I turn away from his door and start walking back home, back down to the Village.